SHARED BY HER LESBIAN BOSS

K.F. JONES

CHAPTER 1

"Are you ready, Amber?"

"Yes, Mistress," Amber confirmed, lifting her head from the pillow to answer. She was naked, and on her knees, face down in the pillows. Her nipples were pressed to the bedsheet, the light friction of the Egyptian cotton stimulating the erect buds.

A slap descended on her bottom. "Not for this, cheeky girl. For the party tomorrow!" Susanna chided.

"Oh, yes, I suppose so, Mistress," Amber said.

"You suppose so? You mean, you don't know?"

"Well, the invitations were quite vague, but I got the impression the guests you invited are all business contacts, and this is an event you regularly host which is why the invitations didn't need details beyond the time and date. I know that all the deliveries you asked me to check on were received and all the guests you invited did confirm they were coming in the end, so I'm sure all that is ready. Sugar, Candy and Pudding haven't said anything about any problems with their preparations, so I assume they're all ready to carry out their roles. I'm sure the evening will go well for you, Mistress," Amber explained.

"Of course, it didn't occur to me that you didn't know about my soirees. You're right, I've invited some of my business contacts, but I've also invited some friends that I don't have business relationships with. Most of my guests are successful people as it happens, but that wasn't why they got invited. Only people I actually like make the list.

"Is it a social occasion then, Mistress?"

"That's the way we think of these events, yes. There's no rule against conducting business though, and I'm always looking for new business relationships and investment opportunities. My guests can do as they please, as long as everyone is happy," Susanna replied as she prowled into position behind Amber.

"I understand, Mistress," Amber said.

Susanna paused, "They can't go in the stables though, of course. There are a couple of guests who are new to the group so if you see them wandering in that direction, be a dear and head them off."

"Yes, Mistress. I'll make sure no-one accidentally disturbs Pepper and Ginger.

"Good," Susanna said, as her hand reached down between Amber's thighs and strong fingers quested for her lips. "You really are ready, aren't you, my dear?"

"Mmm, yes, Mistress," Amber said, pushing herself up and back at Susanna's touch.

After the briefest brush against the outer lips of Amber's sex, Susanna plunged the sizeable dildo she had selected for her harness home in one expert and smooth stroke.

Amber yelped in surprise and approval, her utterances quickly becoming thick with passion. Her guttural groans inflamed her Mistress to thrust harder and faster with each stroke.

It wasn't long before Amber's crescendo was approaching, and the volume of her voice rose in time with it. Susanna changed her pace, slowing right down until the happy noises Amber was making subsided. She continued for a few minutes like that and then suddenly increased the power of her thrusting again.

Once more, Amber's excitement rose, and she felt the approach of a powerful climax, but Susanna denied her again, letting her calm down before bringing her up a third time.

Amber mumbled incoherently, her frustration evident as she realised her Mistress was teasing her with quite deliberate and expert skill. She tried staying silent, biting her lip and concealing her rising excitement, but Susanna always seemed to know when she was close.

After what seemed like an age of torment, Susanna pulled the thick dildo out and took hold of her subs head by the hair, dragging Amber around until the silicone cock waved in front of her face.

"Clean it up, slut," Susanna ordered.

Amber didn't hesitate, she ran her tongue along the length of the toy, lapping up her own juices and making appreciative noises for Susanna's benefit. Then she took the tip in her mouth and began to suck it, bobbing her head up and down as much of the length as she could manage. If Susanna was going to tease her so mercilessly, she would put on a show and see if she could turn the tables.

Her blowjob skills had not been spectacular but had always been popular with her boyfriends, and she used every visually appealing technique she could remember. When Susanna's fingers twined in her hair and began to guide her head, Amber knew she had her rapt attention.

Eventually, though, Susanna pulled back and undid the harness. Amber eagerly awaited the chance to use her tongue to please her Mistress more directly, but her boss ordered her to go to sleep.

Susanna wrapped her soft-skinned limbs around her submissive, spooning her as they drifted off.

"Get a good night of sleep, Amber. Tomorrow will be a busy day," Susanna murmured as Amber's eyes grew heavy.

"Yes, Mistress."

CHAPTER 2

"It's beautiful, Mistress. It looks expensive," Amber said, admiring the black maxi dress Susanna had chosen for her. The wrap front had a plunging neckline that flattered her cleavage wonderfully, and the strappy back matched it. The thigh split gave tantalising glimpses of her recently waxed legs.

"It wasn't cheap, I must say. The sequins give it a wonderful sheen, don't they? Do you like it, my dear?" Susanna asked.

"Oh, yes. Very much," Amber replied, turning to her Mistress with a coy smile. "Does it suit me?"

"It certainly does. I'm sure you'll be turning quite a few heads this afternoon."

"It's going to be quite a fancy do, if I'm dressed like this, and you're wearing that suit," Amber commented.

Susanna turned gracefully on the spot, showing off her outfit. The sequinned jacket was buttoned up, but just enough cleavage was revealed above the blouse, Susanna wore to draw the eye. The leather trousers had sequin accents and laced sides to give a hint of the legs beneath them. Amber thought it a nice touch that their outfits echoed each other, and their matching shoes completed the effect.

"What do you think?" Susanna asked playfully.

Amber licked her lips and drank in the sight of her Mistress, her gaze travelling from the shapely ankles, up her legs and over the swell of her bosom to her dark cherry red lipstick and then those captivating eyes. She grinned and lifted her hands, clawing them in imitation of a cat, "Rawr!"

Susanna laughed, "I'll take that as a sign that you approve."

"Yes, Mistress. You look business-like but sexy at the same time. I can't wait for the party to be over so I can unwrap you and have you all to myself," Amber replied.

"Is that what you think is going to happen?"

"I imagine you'll have me unwrap myself first, but a girl can hope," Amber said with a shrug.

"It's good to have dreams. Now, young lady, my guests will be arriving shortly. Let's go downstairs so we can welcome them," Susanna said, offering her arm. "Come with me, my pet. Accompany your Mistress, so I can show you off."

Amber slipped her arm into the crook of Susanna's, and they walked downstairs side by side.

They waited in one of the large reception rooms, and Amber served chilled fruit juices from the bar for herself and her Mistress while they sat and watched the clock.

When the first guest rang the doorbell, Amber shot to her feet and almost spilt her drink, much to Susanna's amusement. Amber took her Mistress's arm again and accompanied her to the front door.

By the time they entered the hallway, the door was already being opened. As if by magic, a maid had appeared to welcome the guests. Candy was handling the door, and Sugar appeared a moment later to take the guests coats.

Both maids were wearing much more conservative uniforms than they did day to day, Amber noted. The revealing cuts and mini-skirts were gone, and there was nothing obviously risque about their clothes today.

Roxy, Susanna's chauffeur, stepped in first, showing two women in after her. Amber could see more waiting on the porch.

"Baroness Imogen Carruthers and her companion, Charlotte,"

Roxy announced flamboyantly as if presenting people to an old-fashioned ball.

Susanna whispered in Amber's ear, "I must welcome the guests, so please take the coat of the baroness and her companion and the other guests. Sugar and Candy will go and hang them up."

Amber nodded and scurried forward, "Your coat, my Lady," she prompted the Baroness once she was standing behind her. The weather was clement and wearing a coat at all seemed unnecessary, but Amber reached out as the baroness began to remove the coat, helping to slide it down her arms and passing it off to Sugar.

The baroness wasn't tall and had a broad-shouldered figure. She had a pixie cut of dark hair and platinum highlights and wore a finely tailored tweed suit, like a model from a country lifestyle magazine. Baroness Carruthers even had a silver-topped black cane, which seemed to be an accessory rather than an aid to walking.

Amber moved behind the baroness's companion, whatever that meant, and helped lift her full-length cashmere coat up and off her shoulders. Charlotte was shorter than the baroness, perhaps 5'3" if that. As the coat came away, Amber found herself taking a sharp intake of breath.

Charlotte was completely nude under the coat, aside from the black kitten-heeled shoes and the straps that wound up her calves. As she tried not to gape, open-mouthed, Susanna stepped forward and gently took the Baroness's hand. The women performed a side to side air kiss that usually irritated Amber, but she was too distracted by the effort required to avoid staring at the cleft between Charlotte's cheeks or her cute dimples and hourglass figure, to care.

"Good afternoon, Imogen. I'm so pleased you were both able to come. Doesn't Charlotte look lovely today? Are those new shoes?"

"Aye, supposedly they emphasise her calves and buttocks, but mostly they don't make too much noise, and they're comfortable for long periods when she's standing up," the baroness remarked.

"I applaud your practicality, Imogen. So many people forget the finer details like that, what use is a girl who is too sore to stand up?" Susanna said. "We're in the ballroom today," she continued, gesturing down the hallway toward Pudding who was waiting to show people in through the large double doors.

"Thank you, Susanna," Imogen said as she made for the ballroom. Amber couldn't help staring at Charlotte's swaying bottom as she followed after the older woman. Was that a glint of metal that Amber could see as the young woman's bottom moved?

"You're practically drooling, my dear," Susanna whispered in her ear as Roxy fetched the next guest to announce.

"Sorry, Mistress," Amber said, pressing her lips together and turning back to face the front door. "So umm. It's that kind of party then?" she ventured cautiously.

"Of course. I conduct most of my business meetings in the conference rooms in London," Susanna confirmed.

"Yes, Mistress," Amber said meekly. She didn't want to get in trouble, but it was quite clear that she hadn't just been mistaken in assuming that this was a business event. There was a lot more going on than a simple social occasion, Amber realised.

"Dame Cartwright and her companions, Holly and Ivy," Roxy announced, catching Amber's eye and giving her a big wink. Amber felt herself blushing a little and smiled back, hoping the chauffeur didn't notice before she stepped forward to help the Dame out of her coat.

Amber wasn't sure about the style of clothing the tall, imperious looking woman was wearing, a knee-length black leather skirt, white blouse and black jacket didn't really scream a theme to her, at least from behind.

When she took Holly and Ivy's coats and found they were dressed as naughty schoolgirls, she realised that Dame Cartwright was a sexy headmistress. The two girls were of university age at least but were dressed in uniforms. They had kitten-heeled shoes, knee-length white socks, plaid skirts, white blouses and neckties on. Both girls were about 5'4" tall, and their Mistress probably had a good six inches on them,

As Holly and Ivy were introduced to Susanna, Amber got enough of a look to see that the girl's blouses were stretched tightly over their buxom bosoms. The buttons were straining at the material, and ample cleavage was on display. They both wore glasses with thick black rims and had pigtails and bright red lipstick. Holly was a blonde and Ivy a brunette. Amber longed to bury her face in their gorgeous chests and tug at their blouses until the buttons popped off and their heavy breasts sprang free of their constraints.

Instead, she had to content herself with passing the coats to Sugar.

"Emma, so lovely to see you again. Are you still pining for the life of an army colonel or have Holly and Ivy got your mind on other things."

Dame Cartwright boomed out her response in the clear cadence of an army officer, "They are quite exhausting, Susanna. There's no end to their mischief, and they take every ounce of my attention to keep them in line."

"They can't be as much to handle as a class of new recruits, I'm sure?" Susanna remarked.

"Can't they? I think they're worse if anything. Don't let their size fool you. They may be petite, but they're more than a handful," the Dame cautioned.

"You've come to the right place if you need help with them or inventive suggestions, so I'm sure you'll have a wonderful evening," Susanna said, motioning toward the ballroom.

"Oh, I'm sure I will. Someone is bound to be able to give me a pointer that will help," Dame Cartwright said, before leading her girls into the main room.

"Mistress Cauldwell and her companion Diamond," Roxy announced next.

Taking Mistress Cauldwell's coat, she discovered a black latex mini-dress with a plunge that went all the way to the woman's navel and was held fastened by thin chains locked with small heart-shaped padlocks. Regardless, her bosom was barely constrained by the garment and her hips curved generously. The dress had almost no back so everything that wasn't covered by Mistress Cauldwell's long, black and red hair, was tantalisingly exposed.

Diamond was dressed in latex lingerie that left everything covered, but little to Amber's imagination. Both women were heavily tattooed, but with obviously high-quality artwork and taste. Once Diamond's coat was removed, Mistress Cauldwell clipped a leash to the collar around her neck. Amber noted that ankle cuffs and wrist cuffs were an integral part of Diamond's clothing for the afternoon.

Mistress Susanna welcomed the pair, as she had done with the other, glancing at but not speaking to the submissive who apparently didn't warrant a direct conversation, then they were off, spirited into the ballroom.

"Mistress Vanessa Steele and her companion, Jasmine."

"Vanessa, it's been far too long," Susanna said.

"Yes, I'm sorry I've missed a few of your events. My sub took a long term job abroad so that relationship ended. It was a while before a new girl caught my fancy. Jasmine, curtsey for Mistress Susanna," Steele said.

Jasmine, who wore a bondage harness made of leather and seemed to mostly consist of straps and buckles, politely curtseyed to Mistress Susanna, her eyes firmly glued to the floor. Her outfit complimented Mistress Steele's leather corset, trousers and belt that was home to several implements for disciplining her sub.

"Pleased to meet you, Jasmine," Susanna said, acknowledging the sub with a smile and a subtle nod. "Is this her first time at an event like this?"

"Yes, I've been enjoying training her up for it," Vanessa said.

"My new girl, Amber, is also new to the scene. I'm sure this evening will open their eyes to a whole new world," Susanna suggested.

"I'm looking forward to putting Jasmine through her paces in public. She's perhaps a little headstrong, but for me, that makes it all the sweeter when she falls to her knees and submits to my rule," Vanessa said.

"I look forward to seeing her do just that," Susanna replied as Vanessa led her sub toward the ballroom. "I think you'll like this next guest, Amber."

"Yes, Mistress."

CHAPTER 3

Roxy cleared her throat and announced the last couple, "Mistress Yolanda and her companion Zoe."

The final couple struck Amber as rather gothic, even before she removed their pure black coats. Yolanda wore a corset which flattered her figure from her waistline to her cleavage, and a skirt made of leather and lace. Her submissive, Zoe, had a red and black underbust corset on and no blouse.

Zoe's perfect breasts were on display and tipped with pierced nipples that drew Amber's rapt attention so strongly that she barely took in the pale beauty's short gladiator skirt, made of strips of black leather that revealed tantalising glimpses of the girl's body as she moved.

"Yolanda, welcome back to my humble abode," Susanna said.

Yolanda laughed, "It's like a bloody castle, Susanna and far from humble. Most of my friends would kill to live here."

"But not you?"

"Sure, if you ever feel like going over my knee for regular spankings, I'd be delighted to take charge of your estate," Yolanda replied cheekily.

"While I'm sure your spankings are lovely, my dear, I couldn't give up being in charge," Susanna replied.

"Not even temporarily?"

Susanna smiled. "Perhaps. Is that why you come to my parties? In the hopes of giving me a spanking?" Mistress Susanna teased.

Yolanda laughed, "The thought has endless appeal, but you're fishing for compliments, Susanna. You know your parties are the best around, such beautiful surroundings and so many delightful temptations."

"I do try to make my home welcoming."

"Yes, I always feel wanted when I'm here. So does Zoe, I know," Yolanda said, gesturing toward Amber, who looked up at the Mistress's with a guilty expression. "Your new girl is gorgeous, and she can't take her eyes of Zoe's tits, can she?" Yolanda said smugly.

Susanna shook her head, "Amber is a work in progress, I'm afraid. Amber, it's rude to stare. My apologies Yolanda, you must excuse her. I acquired Amber only very recently, and this is her first party."

"It's not a problem, you'd think she'd never seen a pair of boobs before though," Yolanda chuckled huskily, "from the way she's been admiring them."

"Well, one can hardly blame her. I've rarely seen a more exquisitely shaped pair than your Zoe possesses", Susanna said.

"Her tits are close to perfect, aren't they? Of course, she does have the luxury of being young and firm. Zoe will be nineteen next month," Yolanda explained.

"Congratulations. Amber is twenty-three, but you're right, she had never seen boobs used in anger before she came here."

Yolanda looked positively scandalised, "You're pulling my leg. Are you telling me you popped her cherry?"

Amber blushed profusely as the two dommes discussed her virginity so openly. She could feel Zoe giving her curious glances as the women talked.

"With women, at least. Amber hadn't done much more than have a few stray thoughts until I found her," Susanna said, with a hint of obvious pride.

"You lucky thing, it's been years since I got to taste a virgin," Yolanda mused. "Happy days. When I met Zoe about four months ago, she was already well broken in, weren't you, my pet?"

"Yes, Mistress Yolanda," Zoe agreed, her cheeks flushing red.

"I love it when they blush," Yoland said, "it's so sweet and innocent. It's amusing because the things that Zoe can do with that tongue of hers are far from innocent."

Yolanda turned to face Susanna and whispered with a conspiratorial stage whisper, that everyone could hear, "I'm giving serious consideration to collaring her, provided she continues to be a good girl,"

"Really? That's wonderful news. I'm happy for you both," Susanna, catching Amber's eye and her confused expression. "You look puzzled, Amber, what is it?"

"I was wondering why putting a collar on was something to consider," Amber said. Presumably, it had some significance, but she had no idea what.

"My, my. She really is green, isn't she?" Yolanda said.

"Oh, yes. Amber has a lot to learn."

"May I?" Yolanda asked, continuing when Susanna nodded her approval. "There's a world of difference between me putting a collar around Zoe's neck so I can use a leash to control her, or indulge in some pet play or the like and collaring her. In our little community, when we say that we're going to 'collar' someone, what we're talking about is a relationship commitment. If I offer my collar to Zoe and she accepts it, it's a little like an engagement. We even get together to have a little collaring party with friends, just like an engagement party. Does that cover it?" Yolanda checked with Susanna.

"Yes, I think so. Does that satisfy your curiosity, Amber?"

Amber nodded, "Yes, thank you, Mistress. I mean, Mistresses."

The explanation given, Susanna returned to her conversation with her friend, "I see you've had her pierced since we last met," Susanna remarked. "I love the little bat wings on the studs. That's very 'you', Yolanda."

"Oh yes, you've got to have bats or skulls or vampire fangs in my little niche of the world," Yoland chuckled. "I asked her to have it done to see if she was coming along as well as I hoped."

"And I'm guessing, Zoe passed your test with flying colours," Susanna prompted.

"Absolutely. I have a lovely video of her getting pierced. Tell, Mistress Susanna if it hurt you, Zoe."

"It did, Mistress. It hurt a lot, Mistress Susanna," Zoe replied, chewing her lip wistfully as if remembering the experience fondly.

"But she let them do the second one," Susanna said to Yolanda.

"Yes, I'm very proud of her. Zoe took it like a champ. She cried and winced a fair bit, but she didn't try and wimp out of it, did you, darling?"

"No, Mistress."

"They let you film it in the piercing shop?"

Yolanda shook her head, "No, I have a friend, Amaranth, who works in one, but she's quite the sadist. She has a reputation for doing it painlessly in the shop and really knows her stuff. I've used Amaranth for years, and she's done some of my tattoos too. I got her to come over, and we had a little dinner party. Just us, my piercer's sub and a few other friends. Then Zoe got all of her piercings while we all watched and enjoyed the show."

"How wonderful."

"It was. I suspect Zoe's piercings are what was intriguing your sub," Yolanda said shrewdly.

"Is Mistress Yolanda correct, Amber? Were you admiring Zoe's beautiful piercings?"

Amber nodded. "Yes, Mistress. I haven't seen piercings like that up close before."

"You haven't seen them up close now, either," Yolanda smirked.

"Perhaps she should?" Susanna chuckled.

"Zoe, push your chest out, so Amber can really see you show those tits off," Yolanda ordered, before leaning in to whisper something in Susanna's ear.

Susanna smiled. "Amber, come here," she ordered, pointing to a spot beside her.

When Amber was close up against her, Susanna put her lips to her sub's ear, "I need to know if you will consent to what I want from you, today. I want to share you with my friends, as I see fit, with my guests. You have a choice to make. Will you continue to serve me, even if I share you with others, or is this too much for you today?"

Amber swallowed hard and licked her lips, before replying clearly and loudly, "I will serve as you wish, Mistress."

"Good girl. Yolanda, please be my guests. You may direct her as if she were your own for the idea you suggested," Susanna said.

"Smashing," Yolanda said, putting her hand on the back of Amber's head and sweeping her toward Zoe. In a moment, Amber had a close-up view of Zoe's bosom.

"Do you like what you see, Amber?" she purred in Amber's ear.

"Yes, Mistress Yolanda."

"They're delicious, aren't they? So stiff with need. Would you like to lick them?"

Amber nodded. "Yes, please, Mistress."

Yolanda smiled, "You may lick, suck and kiss Zoe's nipples for a short while. Be gentle and kind, I don't want her to suffer at your mouth. Her pain is reserved for my amusement."

Dipping her head, Amber brought her lips to Zoe's pierced doing as she was permitted. She gently probed the erect nubbin with her tongue, delighting in the audible response from the other submissive. Then she tried sucking it gently, playing with the bat-shaped piercing bar that ran horizontally through the coral pink flesh.

"I think Amber likes that," Yolanda commented.

"I think they both seem to," Susanna replied.

"Do you think Amber wants her own piercings? If you want her done, I'm sure Amaranth would do a great job."

"I'm sure she would, I shall discuss it with Amber at some point, but for now, I think I've pushed her far enough."

"Any time you want an introduction just let me know. I can send you the video of Zoe getting pierced if you would like to watch it together with Amber," Yolanda offered.

"Perhaps we will. I would like to see Amber's reaction at least," Susanna mused.

"I think you'd enjoy it. After all Zoe's piercings were done, the night wasn't over," Yolanda said.

"All her piercings?"

Yolanda grinned, "Oh, yes. It's not just her nipples we had done. Her clit hood too. That really brought on the tears but now she loves it, as do I. Zoe totally can't cope with that kind of pain, but it doesn't stop her from enjoying serving me."

"Good for you, how did the rest of the night go?" Susanna enquired.

"Oh you know, just your regular six-way all-girl orgy," Yolanda said with a shrug. "Of course, after Amaranth had gone to so much trouble to come to my house to pierce my beautiful little sub, I had to play the gracious host."

"Well, naturally. Where would civil society be without the basic niceties of hospitality being observed?"

"I assume it would fall apart. Zoe thanked Amaranth with her tongue for quite some time though, so I think the obligations of a host were discharged admirably. Amaranth certainly seemed to be happy," Yolanda said.

"As is only right. Zoe seems to be benefiting greatly from her work, after all."

Yolanda grinned, "Yup. If we let Amber go any longer, the dirty little bitch will be coming all over your hallway." Mistress Yolanda stepped forward and pulled Amber's head away. "That's enough, greedy girls. Anyway, Susanna, Zoe thanked Amaranth, and her sub and my other guests all night. She's been thanking me every day since."

"I would expect nothing less," Susanna said, wiping Amber's sticky mouth with a tissue before she kissed her deeply.

"I think Amaranth would fit right in at your little soirees you know. No pressure, of course, but I'd love to make the introduction," Yolanda suggested.

"Subject to the usual background checks, of course, I'm sure that wouldn't be a problem. If you can email me your friend's details, I'll get that started, and as long as she's cleared, we could all meet up for afternoon tea," Susanna said.

"Great, I'll send you Amaranth's info when I get home. Even if you don't have this girl pierced, I'm sure you'll love her just as much as I do," Yolanda said confidently. "Now, I think we'll go and wait in the ballroom until the others get here."

As Yolanda and her sub walked off, Susanna pulled Amber in for another long kiss, her hands roaming down over Amber's elegant dress. "I cannot wait to get this off you," Susanna growled, nibbling at her sub's ear.

"That sounds good, Mistress," Amber moaned, as strong fingers squeezed her bottom.

"Did you enjoy playing with Zoe?"

"Yes, Mistress."

"Remember your safeword, but I hope you don't use it today. I want you to impress my friends. I can't help being quite proud of how much you've grown in such a short time," Susanna said.

"I'll do my best to impress them, Mistress," Amber said.

"Good, now let's smarten up a little bit. I think I can hear Roxy returning up the drive with the rest of the guests."

Amber stepped back and turned to see the car approaching the turning circle. What would the rest of the guests be like, she wondered.

CHAPTER 4

It hadn't been all that long since Roxy had left after announcing Mistress Yoland and Zoe. Amber was puzzled about how the chauffeur had already managed to pick up more guests, "Mistress, how did they get here so quickly? Didn't she have to go to pick them up from their hotels or something?"

Susanna laughed. "No, we tried that, but it was frustrating. When I got the old gatehouse cleared out, we started to use it as a staging post. The guests arrive and veer off to the car park that's near the gatehouse. Then they can get changed and ready for the party. Roxy brings them to the main house in one of the bigger cars. That way, they arrive at the house fairly quickly, and there aren't lots of stragglers. If you let people turn up on their own, half the people arrive mid-orgy, and that can be a bit tedious."

"Orgy? Wow. To think I thought this was going to be a business event until I took that first coat," Amber said.

"I did wonder. That's why I kept you away from the details, once I got the idea you thought this was some kind of business schmoozing dinner party, I told everyone to play up to that," Susanna said, grinning wickedly.

"Well, I failed that test, didn't I?" Amber said grumpily.

Susanna gave her a friendly fist bump to the shoulder, "It was just a bit of a practical joke, no harm done. Sugar and Candy have been having terrible trouble keeping a straight face."

"I might have known they'd enjoy keeping me in the dark," Amber grumbled.

Susanna imitated Sugar's voice, "Ohhh, the caterers don't like it when people go in the dining hall and disturb things."

"That sounded perfectly sensible to me!" Amber protested.

"That does happen actually, they like to know they can get the job done and not be criticised for something the hosts changed like moving the tables and mucking up the seating chart. But in this case, it was because we wanted to set-up the ballroom for the party, not for catering," Susanna said.

"But I saw their vans, and they were unloading lots of boxes and stuff. They had half a dozen people lugging stuff around," Amber said. The doors were pushed open again, and the new guests arrived.

"You'll see," was all Susanna said before Roxy announced the first person.

Amber had to stew as she removed coats and passed them to the maids, admiring each new guest's sense of style. The dominants certainly liked to dress up, and each had their own unique look, albeit with certain themes running through their outfits.

A lot of the fetish clothing that the guests and their submissives wore was custom-made. There was leather, lace, PVC and latex in abundance and, of course, a lot of collars, cuffs and buckles. Amber had never seen the like of it, even having lived in Susanna's mansion for a while now.

Amber marvelled at how beautiful and varied the ladies attending were. Susanna's friends ranged from the classically beautiful like Zoe, who could easily have been a model, to the Baroness who was butch through and through. The Baroness had set Amber's mind racing, and her non-traditional style hadn't felt out of place at all or been off-putting.

One of the dommes had arrived dressed as a pirate queen, thankfully sans parrot, but she did have two comely sailor wenches, dressed like something out of a swashbuckling film. Another had two girls who wore cat ears and once they took off their coats, revealed cat-tails attached to butt plugs, just like Pepper and Ginger wore.

They had dropped to all fours when their Mistress attached clips to their collars, and they'd assumed their personas as kittens. Then they'd crawled across the hard floor of the hallway into the bathroom, their Mistress following after them holding gripping their fine leather leashes in one fist. Amber didn't like to ask if it was a bit out of character for a kitten to accept a collar and leash and if that wasn't more like a dog.

"Roxy, is that everyone?" Susanna asked, frowning slightly.

"Yes, Mistress. Everyone who was at the guest house."

"Amber, check the list for me."

Amber picked up the clipboard from a nearby table and ticked off the names one by one. "Mistress Chevalier is the only one missing, Mistress."

Susanna rolled her eyes. "Of course, she would be," she sighed.

"Mistress, do you think she'll be very late?" Amber asked.

"Probably not, she's just a bit disorganised with this sort of thing. She has a tendency to lose track of time. It's not deliberate."

"Should we wait for her, Mistress?" Roxy asked.

"We'll give her another ten minutes. I should probably have called her myself this morning to chivvy her along," Susanna admitted. "Sugar, Candy, go and start serving drinks and make sure the rest of the guests are happy. Please tell them we may be a few minutes. Pudding you can get back the kitchen if you need to."

The rest of the staff dispersed, leaving Roxy and Amber with Mistress Susanna.

"Is there anything we can do for you, while we wait?" Roxy asked.

"Hmmm. Would you like to kiss Amber, perhaps?" Susanna replied.

"If it would please you, Mistress," Roxy said, advancing on Amber. "Come here, slut," the chauffeur said gruffly, pulling Amber in and taking her mouth, much as Mistress Susanna did when she wanted to claim her.

Amber felt herself wilting in Roxy's grip. She was strong and held tight to her, as Amber's knees went weak, shaking from the sensation that was so like being kissed by her boss. Roxy was hungry, animalistic and passionate. Amber could hear Mistress Susanna behind her, giving words of encouragement. Not to Amber though, she was prompting Roxy, telling her to control Amber, to own her lips and tongue, to savour the moment.

"Yes, this is definitely better than checking my phone for social media updates," Susanna mused. "You two look good together. Perhaps I should have made this happen sooner."

"You should have," Roxy replied, taking a break from her exploration of Amber's tongue. "This slut is delightful."

Amber was shocked. Not at being described as a slut but a woman she was attracted to, but by the overly familiar way that Roxy was speaking to Susanna. It seemed disrespectful, in a way that she, Candy, Sugar or Pudding wouldn't have dared.

Roxy seemed to have a different dynamic with their Mistress than Amber or the maids did, and that made her immediately curious about their relationship.

"Isn't she though? I seem to remember a certain scepticism on your part when Amber first arrived," Susanna replied.

Roxy shrugged and kissed Amber again for a moment, before replying. "I can't be right all the time. You've done an excellent job with her. To think, she was a virgin less than a month ago, and now she's at her first all-girl orgy. Mistress, you are a genius with new girls," Roxy said.

"Flattery will get you everywhere, Roxy."

"I certainly hope so."

"I think I hear a vehicle approaching so we'll have to resume this another time, but can I take it that you'd be keen to have a more involved play session with Amber, Roxy?"

Roxy wiped her mouth and nodded. Then she did something that surprised Amber, given their interaction so far. The chauffeur dropped to her knees, crawling over to the chair that Susanna had sat in, she looked up at their domme from between her legs.

"Yes, Mistress. I would like to serve at your pleasure alongside Amber, whenever you wish me to do so," Roxy confirmed, her voice thick with lust.

Susanna reached down and gently cupped Roxy's face in one hand, "I'm sure that can be arranged, my darling. Perhaps next week we can find enough time to fulfil your needs, hmm?"

"Thank you, Mistress," Roxy said, her head bowing as she kissed Susanna's outstretched hand subserviently.

"Good girl. Now, stand up, it's time for us to welcome my last guest," Susanna ordered.

CHAPTER 5

Amber watched as the mud-splattered Land Rover pulled around the turning circle and disappeared out of view toward the tradesman's entrance. It was towing a large horsebox.

"Is that her?" Amber asked.

"Yeah, that's Mistress Chevalier, alright," Roxy with resignation.

"Come on, we may as well go and meet her at the side door," Susanna said, hurrying off with an exasperated look on her face.

"I'm guessing that's not her real name unless the horsebox is a gigantic coincidence."

"No, she's quite horsey, but her real name is Xanthippe Jade Marshall," Roxy whispered as they followed after Susanna.

"What?" Amber hissed back.

"I'm not kidding."

"Xanthippe?"

"Named after the wife of Socrates. Most of us call her Mistress Chevalier, of course," Roxy said. "She goes by Jade among our betters."

"I'm not surprised."

"Enough chatter you two," Susanna ordered before opening the door and going out into the yard.

Mistress Chevalier had already parked and was about to open the rear of the horsebox.

"What ho!" she called out when she saw Susanna.

"You're late, Jade," Susanna said crossly.

"Sorry, I was working on a particularly tricky commission and time got away from me. You know me, I'd forget to eat if someone didn't tell me it was lunchtime," the ruddy-faced replied.

"Really, Jade. There are lots of calendars and reminder apps and all sorts of ways to be organised these days. Everyone has had to wait for you."

Jade had the good grace to look sheepish. "Sorry old bean didn't mind to cause you grief. I do have something I think you'll want to see, though. Can I get some help with this?" the jodhpur wearing woman asked.

Susanna gestured, and Roxy stepped forward to help lower the door, which became a ramp. Amber was glad that she hadn't been picked as she didn't have a clue about this sort of thing.

"Who's the new girl?" Jade asked over her shoulder.

"Her name is Amber, she's my personal assistant," Susanna answered.

"Do you like ponies, Amber?" Jade asked.

Amber shrugged. "I don't really know much about horses."

Jade guffawed at that, in the kind of hearty way that genuine country gentlewomen had about them. "No, not horses, you silly girl. Ponies. Haven't you met Ginger and Pepper yet? Really, Susanna, you shouldn't keep your girls so isolated in that big house. You are a terror for forgetting to introduce people."

"I'm forgetful? Oh, you've got some nerve Jade Marshall," Susanna grumbled.

"Come on up, Amber. Don't worry, just hitch up your skirts, so they don't snag. It's perfectly clean in here," Jade called from within the horsebox.

Amber glanced at Susanna for permission, then made her way up the ramp.

"Amber, meet my new pony, Victoria. Vicky for short. Isn't she a sight to behold?" Jade said proudly.

Victoria was indeed a sight to behold. She was at least six feet tall and had a long plait of platinum blonde hair trailing down her back. Her feet were encased in knee-length hoof boots, which imitated the shape of a horse's hoof, by having her almost on tiptoes.

A complicated leather harness wrapped around her body, with straps passing between her legs, and over and under her shoulders. Her large breasts were mostly unobstructed but did have large bar piercings through her nipples and black leather straps over and under them, emphasising their size and shape.

Vicky's head was encased in a harness with a rubber bit gag between her teeth and blinders on, as well as a bridle hanging down behind her head. A prominent tail was jutting from between her cheeks, and Amber could only imagine the butt plug that was buried in Vicky's bottom.

All of this was similar to the kind of tack and harness she'd seen Mistress Susanna use on her ponygirls, Pepper and Ginger. There was one difference, and it was big. Not only was Amber tall, but her stomach showed if not a full six-pack, the clear indications of strong muscle and low body fat. Her thighs were thick and muscular, and her shoulders were similarly rounded with muscle.

Vicky wasn't the most extreme female bodybuilder that Amber had ever seen, in pictures at least. She was softer and less lean than the professionals, but Amazonian would have been an apt description.

"What do you think?" Jade asked excitedly.

"I'm no expert, Mistress Chevalier but Vicky seems like a lovely pony. She's very impressive," Amber replied, trying not to say the wrong thing.

"I call her a Shire Pony, because she's such a fine physical specimen and I can work her as hard as I like," Mistress Chevalier said, as she led the young woman down the ramp.

"What do you think, Susanna?" Mistress Chevalier asked, expectantly.

Susanna's eyes widened in surprise when she saw the huge ponygirl, but she soon got herself under control and approached to get a closer look. Her hand reached out, but she stopped herself before she touched the pony and looked at Jade to ask for permission, "May I?"

"Of course. Vicky loves to be touched, don't you, my pet?" Jade said, stroking the shoulder of the much taller woman.

Vicky stamped her foot in confirmation and whinnied. Susanna reached out and stroked the woman's shoulder, then down her side, all the day to her strong thigh. Vicky shivered in response to the light touch.

"She's amazing, Jade. Is she quick?"

"Oh yes, she's got quite some pace on her, and she can pull hard, of course," Jade agreed.

"Does she respond well to the whip? She looks pretty tough," Susanna asked.

Mistress Chevalier chuckled, a dirty sound if Amber had ever heard one. "Want to find out?"

Susanna blinked. "I meant, in a race."

Vicky's domme shook her head gently, passing Susanna a riding crop. "Yes, but I'll only answer if you test her mettle yourself."

"We should probably get inside."

"Probably, but lighten up a little, Susanna. If we go inside now, everyone will want to play with Vicky, don't you think?"

"I'm sure she's going to turn heads, she's rather special," Susanna agreed.

"Yes, she is. Believe me, I'm happy to have found her. Now, are you going to crop her bottom and see how she responds or are you going to be a spoilsport?" Jade teased.

Susanna shot Jade a dark glance and Amber realised she was chewing her lip, hoping to see the crop in action and what Vicky's response might be to it. "Jade, you are quite simply, impossible," Susanna hissed. But her objection didn't stop her counting out all six strikes of the crop she applied to Vicky's left buttock.

Amber swallowed, her throat dry as Vicky whimpered. The pony might not have responded how Susanna or Jade would like, but Amber could certainly feel her own mounting arousal as she watched Vicky receive her discipline.

Susanna reached out with her left hand, flattening her fingers against Vicky's strong stomach. Then she turned her head to face Jade, who merely grinned lasciviously as Susanna's hand quested down over the smooth flesh of Vicky's abdomen.

When her Mistress licked her lips, with just the tip of her tongue, and Vicky whinnied, Amber felt her arousal spike. A moment later, Susanna lifted her fingers and inspected the glistening moisture that coated them. Susanna lifted her right hand, crop clenched in her fist, and uncurled her index finger to beckon Amber forward.

Amber moved to her Mistress's side, and soon Susanna's wet fingers were sucked between her lips. The taste of Vicky's arousal filled her mouth as she greedily sucked her boss's fingers clean.

"Now that, is sexy," Mistress Chevalier breathed. "What do you think, Susanna?"

"I think Vicky likes the whip, a lot."

Jade nodded. "Yes, yes, she does. Instant wetness. It does help her pace as well since you asked. She's a great all-rounder."

"Good. Glad to hear it. Congratulations. Now, shall we join the party?"

"I have my stuff to unpack still," Jade reminded Susanna.

Susanna sighed. "Of course. I wish you'd come earlier. Amber, Roxy, Mistress Chevalier has some of her products that are going to need taking inside so she can display them. Some of the ladies might want to make purchases."

Turning to Amber, Susanna gave her an appraising look. "I love that dress on you, and there's a certain appeal to seeing you filthy, covered in mud with a torn dress but that's not the theme for today, and it's an expensive indulgence. You can strip off now, Amber and serve Mistress Chevalier in the nude, which I'm sure everyone else will enjoy."

Amber began to strip off without a word, blushing as Mistress Chevalier wolf-whistled and applauded loudly. She carefully took the dress inside and made sure it was safely stowed away where it wouldn't get dirty. Amber took her expensive shoes off as well, and returned to the horsebox entirely nude, as ordered.

"There you go, Jade. Please try and be quick with this, I want you at the party before we start properly. I'll send Sugar and Candy to help too," Susanna said.

"Thanks, Susanna. I appreciate it, just a few more loyal customers would be a big help. I'm sorry, I was late. I promise I'll make it up to you," Mistress Chevalier said.

"Good, because if you do it again, I'll give you such a spanking!" Susanna said, then stuck her tongue out at Jade and turned to leave.

Jade laughed, "Darling, you can bend me over and spank me any time you want."

Susanna stopped dead in her tracks and took a deep breath. "Noted," she said before she hurried off.

"Oh dear, Mistress Chevalier, I think you're going to get it good and hard later," Roxy opined.

"I do hope so, dear. Oh, don't look so scandalised. I may have a preference for topping girls like you but doesn't mean I don't like a good hard spanking now and then. Especially in front of my peers," Mistress Chevalier said with a hearty wink. Roxy laughed.

With that, they set about emptying the ponygirl tack that Mistress Chevalier explained were her business. She specialised in high-end leather goods and other equipment for people into pony play and similar things. Her boxes of goods were full of riding crops, bridles, body harnesses, bit gags and more delightful things.

By the time they were done, Amber was glistening with perspiration. Mistress Chevalier looked her up and down as she took deep breaths to catch up, clearing enjoying what she was looking at. "You look scrumptious after a little light exercise, Amber. I could lick you all over and eat you right up. Have you tried pony racing?" she asked.

"Yes. I raced Mistress earlier in the week, and Pepper and I won," Amber said sheepishly.

"I sense a but coming?"

"I got in trouble for it."

"You got in trouble just for winning? That's not like Susanna," Jade pointed out.

"No, for telling Pepper I'd give her an orgasm if she could win. Apparently, that wasn't in the spirit of the thing, but I didn't know that" Amber said.

"You loved your punishment though, I'll bet," Jade commented, chuckling when Amber's blushing confirmed her guess. "Anyway, I didn't mean racing with you as the driver. I meant you'd look gorgeous if you worked up a good sweat pulling a trap."

"Agreed," Roxy interjected. Vicky whinnied and stamped her foot to add her endorsement.

"Thank you, that's very kind," Amber said.

"Not a bit of it, I'm just a filthy old mare who loves to see a young filly hot and sweaty," Jade said.

"But you're not old," Amber protested.

"Kind of you to say so, and it was just a figure of speech. I'm the oldest here, but I keep myself in good shape. Well, until you compare me to someone like Vicky of course, who spends a ludicrous amount of time on her health and fitness. Not that I don't appreciate that, of course, it looks great on her and giving her enough exercise to break a sweat gets me all the exercise I need," Jade said with a dirty laugh.

"You seem to be in much better shape than me, Mistress Chevalier," Amber pointed out. "You didn't get out of breath moving this stuff."

"You work in an office, I'm making and moving leather all day. If Susanna wants you to get some more exercise though, I'm sure Vicky and I would be happy to help," Jade said, earnestly, before giving another delightfully filthy laugh.

"I live to serve, Mistress Susanna," Amber replied, coyly.

"Translation, I hope Mistress Susanna shares me with you, Mistress Chevalier," Roxy scoffed.

"That sounds fun," Mistress Chevalier said. "Come on, we've done enough. Let's go and get the party started, shall we?"

"Yes, Mistress," chorused Roxy and Amber, with an agreeable whinny from Vicky.

CHAPTER 6

When Amber had last wandered into the ballroom, it had been a largely empty room, the only things that drew the eye were on the wall. A grand fireplace against one wall and even two smaller ones and paintings. There were paintings everywhere. They were all old and looked like they'd come with the house, just like the wood panelling and polished oak floor.

The change since she'd last been here was immediately noticeable. For the most part, it was the additional furniture which drew the eye. Around the edges of the room, Chesterfield style leather seating had been placed. There were right-angled sofas in each corner big enough for a group to sit on, and big 3-seater straight sofas along the long walls, with a handful of chaise longues as well.

Near each of the main seats, a footstool had been placed, and each of those was several feet long, big enough to lay down on if your feet were on the floor. It was all a rich oxblood red, the creases of the leather darkening to an almost black colour.

A series of huge and thick black rugs had been used to carpet most of the floor, protecting the well-polished oak from the feet of the furniture and presumably, the knees of any submissives ordered to them. One area was free of rugs because it had been covered instead with thick exercise mats that interlocked like a jigsaw puzzle.

Next to them was an area that had been covered in plastic sheeting, because what looked like a large inflatable paddling pool had been placed there. There was a table by it, covered with thick towels and bottles of baby oil, which Amber really wanted to see in use. Oiled up submissives wrestling each other? That had to be something she'd get to see, it just had to be.

Then there was another ring of furniture, but not in the classic vein of a country house. These items were more modern, constructed from heavy, wood stained black, wrought iron and shining steel. Where these items were upholstered, they'd been covered in the same oxblood leather as the Chesterfield sofas.

The inner ring was all far more specialist than the outer ring. There were three St Andrew's crosses, used for restrained a submissive upright and spreadeagled for play or punishment. They were joined by several spanking benches and a matching pillory, a modern take on a medieval favourite. Amber licked her lips as she imagined her head and wrists being clamped in one of those, while her body was on display and accessible to the room full of dominant women and their submissives. She shivered in anticipation of what might happen.

There were two cages, currently unoccupied, one a low style a submissive would need to be on all fours to occupy that had a coffee table on top, the other a tall one with cuffs dangling from the top bars to allow a girl to be displayed standing upright.

A hefty looking frame supported an arrangement of straps and padded supports that Amber recognised as a sex swing from a bawdy comedy film she'd gone to see with friends. Next to it, was a boxy-looking leather chair which seemed innocent at first glance, until you see the thick leather wrist and ankle straps on the arms and legs that could restrain a subject for interrogation.

It was no wonder Mistress Susanna had hired the furniture for the party, rather than owning it outright. Not that Amber thought she couldn't afford it, but it would hardly be practical to store this much furniture without having a dedicated room for it.

Mistress Susanna's guests were distributed around the room, lounging on sofas with their subs at their feet or standing, sipping wine and stroking the head of a submissive who was kneeling beside them.

In the centre of the room, a shallow stage had been assembled. Low enough to step on to easily and high enough to make the occupants easy to see. Mistress Susanna stood up there, waiting as her guests chatted.

"Ah, I see our final guest has officially arrived," Susanna said, her voice cutting through the conversation around her, which soon faded away. "Good, now we can begin. Amber, please join me on stage."

Mistress Susanna gestured around her, "Welcome to my humble abode, one and all. For those of you who don't know, or are new to these events and for anyone who might have forgotten, I must go over some ground rules."

"There are buffet tables in the dining room next door, and plenty of drink options and nibbles. I ask that everyone remain sober for the whole event, and I regret that if anyone is intoxicated, they'll have to leave. Please be respectful of the furniture, in particular the items outside of this room. Much of it is as old as the house and quite valuable," Susanna said, pointing at a marble-topped side table near one of the hearths.

"The group safeword for this evening is 'Cotswold', but please remember to be mindful of any other strange words a submissive may blurt out that could be their normal safeword. If in doubt, as you already know, pause your play and check. The kitchen is strictly off-limits. Pudding is an excellent cook, and none of us wants her disturbed or our evening meal will not be up to her high standards," Susanna said, "not to mention the spanking she would give a transgressor would leave them unable to stand for a week!" The audience was clearly familiar with Pudding's cooking and her predilection for turning bottoms hot pink.

"As you can see, I have provided an excellent selection of furniture for you to use, as well as a collection of instruments and toys. On the table by the hallway door is a bowl with some keys in it. These unlock bedrooms upstairs, which you may use at your discretion. If you want privacy, you may lock the door, and put the 'Do not disturb' sign on it, but an unlocked room is in open invitation to other guests that you would like more company, for play or voyeurism. Please don't hog the rooms all night if you must use them."

Amber looked around the room while Susanna talked, watching how the guests responded to the speech. Plenty of them caught her gaze as she looked at them, and she could feel other eyes on her, admiring her nakedness. She straightened her back a bit and pulled her shoulders back, making sure her figure was displayed well and enjoying the twinkling in the eyes of the guests as they sized her up like a piece of meat.

"I want to encourage you all to avoid the bedrooms, and instead, play in public in here, so that we can all enjoy the sights and sounds of each other's pleasure," Susanna said, "or pain. I think that covers everything."

"Who's the new girl, Susanna," Mistress Cauldwell asked.

"Of course, silly me. Everyone, this is Amber, my new personal assistant," Susanna explained.

"Is she one of us, or a submissive?" Mistress Cauldwell asked.

"As you might guess from her state of undress, Amber is also one of my submissives," Susanna confirmed.

"Are you sure? She doesn't look very deferential to me. She looks quite proud and defiant," Mistress Cauldwell said, "Diamond here is kneeling and ready to serve." The domme used the leash wrapped around her fist to destabilise Diamond's position and pull her off balance. The girl fell to the rug beneath her, and when the leash was relaxed, resumed her kneeling position without complaint, despite the fire that Amber saw flashing in her eyes.

"I'm quite sure," Susanna said. "What is it you all want, a demonstration of Amber's submission to my will?"

Amber wondered if it was improved or if it was pre-arranged but either way, her Mistress was clearly enjoying putting on a show. The audience was enjoying themselves too calling out encouragement and agreeing with Mistress Cauldwell.

"Kneel before me, Amber," Susanna ordered. When she did so, her Mistress called out to the crowd, "Is this what you? To be entertained?"

"Yes!" came the response. "More!" the ladies shouted.

"Amber, who do you serve?"

"I serve you, Mistress."

"A month ago, had you been with a woman before?"

"No, Mistress."

"Had you been spanked? Or caned?"

"No, Mistress."

"Turn to face the audience, and touch yourself," Susanna ordered.

Amber shuffled around and spread her knees apart, obediently slipping a hand between her thighs to stroke her wet lips.

"If I told you to lick my pussy in front of my guests, would you, Amber?" Susanna asked.

"Yes, Mistress. I would love to," Amber gasped.

Susanna crouched close behind Amber, tugging her head back and kissing her neck, slipping a hand around and pinching her nipple hard until Amber couldn't help but cry out. "Amber, if I told you to walk across the room, and drop to your knees before one of my guests, then worship their pussy until they come, would you do it?"

"For you, anything, Mistress!" Amber cried out.

"Stop touching yourself and lick your fingers clean, slowly," Susanna ordered. Amber was frustrated from being denied a climax but did as she was told and supported her Mistress as well as she could. She made her display of submission as wanton as possible, licking and sucking her fingers wetly and with evident pleasure. The audience watched her with rapt attention and evident approval.

"Ladies, Amber was completely new to the scene when I found her and I've been training her hard for weeks. I am the only dominant who has had the pleasure of her. Should I share her with you? Would anyone like that?" Susanna asked.

The response was a huge cheer and a chorus of agreement.

"The vote is clear, and I shall abide by your wishes, as the gracious host that I am. Now, who shall I choose to have the services of my latest girl, I wonder?" Susanna pondered, looking out at the assembled dommes. "Perhaps our most august members, the Baroness or Dame Cartwright would like a turn? Or perhaps you would like to sample Amber yourself, Mistress Cauldwell."

"Everyone in here wants her, Susanna," Baroness Carruthers replied.

"Of course we do, make your choice so we can all have some fun," Dame Cartwright echoed with a hearty laugh.

Susanna pretended to ponder the decision for just a few moments longer, teasing the crowd expertly. Amber was bursting to know who she would be given too as well. Between her thighs, her arousal was keenly felt, and she could imagine that spending time with any of the dominant women in the room would be nothing short of amazing.

Finally, when the tension was unbearable, Susanna announced her choice, "Mistress Chevalier, despite your tardiness, would you accept the offer of being the second domme to break in my newest acquisition?"

Mistress Chevalier looked quite taken aback, coughing on the sausage roll she had been happily eating, and thumping her chest to clear her throat. "Me?" she asked with obvious disbelief.

"Yes, Jade. You. I would like to offer you the full services of Amber for the afternoon. Does that sound good?" Susanna asked.

"Umm. Well, I'm flattered, and yes, it does sound good. Thank you," Mistress Chevalier replied. "I do need to finish setting up a few things first, though."

Susanna shook her head, "No, that's alright, take Amber with you, I'm sure she can help you with that, as well as any other needs you might have. Ladies, as a special treat, Mistress Chevalier has brought along some of her wares to show off. As you probably know, Jade is a highly regarding saddler and harness maker who provides leather goods to the ponygirl community, in particular. She also makes many items for more general play and takes custom orders. I can personally recommend her services as a leatherworker. Later on, when the goods are set up in the other room, you'll be able to take a good look and purchases or place orders as you see fit."

The news was met with a good deal of approval, and Amber noticed that Mistress Chevalier looked quite relieved at the positive response. leather goods and speciality items for you to look at and either purchase or place

"Enjoy Amber, Jade, she's rather good at taking orders, as you'll soon discover."

"I'm sure we'll get along famously, Susanna. Would you be able to look after Vicky while I'm otherwise engaged?" Mistress Chevalier asked.

"I'd be delighted to."

"Please, use her as you see fit. She too is good at taking orders," Mistress Chevalier replied, "and she's happy to be on display. Victoria is something of a show pony, you see."

"I'll make sure to give everyone something to appreciate then, Jade. Thank you. Run along with Mistress Chevalier now, Amber and make me proud," Mistress Susanna said.

"Yes, Mistress," Amber said as she stood up and followed the Mistress from the room.

CHAPTER 7

Amber was hot and sweaty again by the time she'd finished unpacking the boxes and moving the tables around and laying out Mistress Chevalier's products. The whips and paddles were easily dealt with, but the saddles and some small items of furniture and display stands were more cumbersome.

Mistress Chevalier barely lifted a finger to help her; instead, she sat back and gave instructions as Amber did the physical work. The older woman was having the time of her life, sometimes making her move a heavy saddle several times before she liked the position.

Amber had asked what type of horses the saddles were for and been roundly mocked. The saddles were designed purely for human ponies, to be worn when they were on all ours and allowing them to be ridden. They were far lighter than horse saddles, and not all subs could support their Mistress and move much. Mistress Chevalier said it was more about roleplay, although she had found that Vicky was so unusually strong, she could easily crawl around the room, carrying her domme on her back.

"I'll say it again, Amber. You look beautiful with your skin shining with sweat. Come here, sit on my lap so I can get a closer look,"

Mistress Chevalier said. "Straddle me," she ordered, having Amber positioned face to face with her, on the footstool, she was perched on.

Once she was in position, Mistress Chevalier stroked her hands up Amber's thighs, up her ribcage and then cupped her damp breasts in her palms. "You are truly stunning," the domme said before she dipped her head and licked a line up between Amber's breasts, then over to her left nipple. She licked and sucked there for a while, before tasting her other nipple.

"You're delicious. I could definitely eat you all up," Jade confirmed.

"Thank you, Mistress. That feels so good," Amber replied.

"I suppose I still have some skills, despite being so old," Jade laughed.

Amber shook her head, "You're not old, Mistress Chevalier. You're beautiful and sexy."

"Well, that's very kind of you to say dear, but I'm sure a young slip of a thing would have been much more excited at the prospect of being shared with one of Susanna's other friends," Mistress Chevalier demurred. "There are far younger, prettier dommes than me here today."

"Not at all. I don't wish to speak out of turn, but you seem much more approachable and, well, fun than some of the other guests," Amber said.

Mistress Chevalier laughed heartily at that. "Oh, I do, do I?"

"Yes, you do," Amber agreed firmly.

"Perhaps my pleasures aren't to your taste, though. I'm surprised that Susanna hasn't had you in harness yet. Do you not relish the thought of being a pony for your Mistress?"

Amber shrugged. "I haven't been here long, Mistress. There hasn't been much time to think about it, or to try it."

"You'll have plenty of time with Susanna I'm sure. I cannot imagine her giving up a submissive so thoroughly delightful and easy on the eye," Mistress Chevalier said.

"Thank you, Mistress. Would you like me to serve you in some way?" Amber asked, her tongue subconsciously licking her lip, "I will do as I'm told, of course."

"I'm sure that would be lovely, but I wouldn't want to cross any boundaries you have," Mistress Chevalier said.

Amber giggled. "Is there something really naughty you'd like me to do? It's ok to tell me, if there is," she teased.

"Minx. I'm not sure how naughty the things I like would seem to you, but I don't want to shock you, all the same," Mistress Chevalier said.

"I'm sure you won't, Mistress. Would you like to ask me about something, and see what I think?" Amber suggested.

"Fine. Since you insist. How do you respond to pain?"

"Quite well, I suppose. I've been brought to tears and managed to cope with that since I got here," Amber said proudly.

The dominant had a little half-smile at that comment. "Have you indeed? That's interesting. What I really wondered though was whether pain had you getting wet in places your tears didn't run?"

Amber dipped her head and stared into Mistress Chevalier's eyes, "It has done, yes. Would that please you?"

Mistress Chevalier didn't reply, she reached up and pulled Amber down into a long kiss, her hands exploring the younger woman's body all the while. When the kiss finally broke, the dommes mouth dipped to Amber's right nipple, and her fingers found the left.

Slowly at first, Amber's world blossomed with pleasurable sensations as the older domme licked and sucked at one nipple while stroking and teasing the other with her fingers. Then the gentle manipulations grew firmer, more insistent. The teeth nipped at her sensitive flesh, and the fingers pinched and tugged. Amber gave a low moan, and that spurred Mistress Chevalier on.

The fingers on her left nipple shifted, taking a good grip and then combining a tight pinch, with a twisting and tugging motion. Amber's head tipped back, and she squealed, loud enough that she half-expected someone to come running. Mistress Chevalier chuckled triumphantly, her amusement muffled by the wet nipple in her mouth, which she proceeded to bite hard, causing another burst of pain.

A hand slid down between Amber's thighs, and the strong fingers of someone who worked with her hands delved between her sopping wet lips, quickly finding her clit. Amber felt the wave of pleasure begin to swell as her swollen clitoris was expertly played with, then she felt the sting of tears filling her eyes when Mistress Chevalier pinched her sensitive nub as well.

"You're sopping wet, you naughty girl," Mistress Chevalier said. "Come for me, Amber. Come from my gift of pain."

Amber wanted to resist, as the domme manipulated her nipples and clit with her mouth and tongue, but it was far from easy. Gradually she felt her passion rising, despite the intense pain she was being tormented with.

"Are you fighting it, you hot little bitch?" Mistress Chevalier growled.

"Yes, Mistress," Amber groaned, holding her release back with all her willpower.

"You won't win. You're too much of a slut not to give in to your filthy thoughts," Mistress Chevalier insisted, between bites of her nipples and pinches of her clitoris. "You'll get off on the pain despite yourself, I can tell. Girls like you get so wet when you torment them, and they come like fountains."

"No. I won't, Mistress," Amber claimed boldly, but was soon disproven as she rushed over the peak of her first climax and straight into a second, shuddering and gasping and calling out Mistress's name, "Jade, oh, Jade!"

Wet fingers were pushed into her mouth a moment later for her to suck clean and she tasted herself on Mistress Chevalier's fingers. A sharp slap landed on her thigh, "That's for being disrespectful and not using the title I've earned."

"I'm sorry, Mistress. I meant no disrespect, I promise," Amber moaned.

"I warned you that you couldn't resist my touch," the older domme said, before pulling her head down and passionately kissing her, tasting Amber's pussy from her lips. "I've been playing these games since I was your age. I started serving older women when I was a fresh young university student, and I've never stopped playing since. Once I would have been the one serving the pleasures of a woman twice my age. Then I changed roles, and now the sluts serve me. Worshipping me. I've had more pussy than you can dream of so when I tell you to come, you're going to come, my girl, whether you want to resist or not."

Defeated, sweaty and used, Amber nodded. "Yes, Mistress. I'm sorry for fighting."

Mistress Chevalier laughed, "Don't be, my girl. Do you think I'd have taken on Vicky, with her great big muscles and such long legs, if I didn't relish a challenge?"

"Did I make you happy, Mistress?" Amber asked.

"Why don't you feel me and find out?" Mistress Chevalier suggested, then took hold of her hand and pressed it into her lap. Amber gasped. Below the material of the dominant woman's jodhpurs was a distinctly unladylike bulge. The woman chuckled at her reaction and pulled her in tight, "Get it out."

Fumbling blindly, with their torso pressed together and little room for her to move her hand, Amber sought the buttons of the jodhpurs even as she whimpered at the thought of it. The cock she had felt was swelling, as she tried to free it. Amber felt confused, disoriented by the unexpectedly phallic contents of Mistress Chevalier's riding trousers, but when the woman gave her more room, easing back on the hug, she was able to open the buttons and release the stiffening member within.

"Good girl," Mistress Chevalier said, pushing her roughly off her lap and to the fall.

Amber fell back and looked up, startled by the move. Jutting from Mistress Chevalier's lap was a large, purple and crimson cock. The silicone was detailed, with veins on the shaft and a big mushroom head. Mistress Chevalier's hand was resting on a bulb strapped in place at her side, and a thin tube disappeared toward her crotch. It was inflatable, which was a relief to realise.

"That gave you a shock, didn't it?" Mistress Chevalier laughed.

Amber blushed, then giggled. "Yes, Mistress. I didn't know what to think."

"Have I lost you entirely, or are we still playing?"

Amber took a deep breath, "We're still playing, Mistress. Until Mistress Susanna takes me back."

"Good girl, then up, and on your knees, and give my big boy a good suck, won't you? Make it nice and whorish for me," Mistress Chevalier ordered confidently.

Amber found the cock buried in her mouth, as deep as she could take it. The swollen girth stretched her jaw, and the head came close to choking her. All the while Mistress Chevalier called her vulgar names and demanded that she redouble her efforts. Amber could feel her inner thighs were getting coated in dribbles of her arousal.

"Enough, on all fours so I can fuck you, Amber," Mistress Chevalier ordered.

The cock buried in her to the hilt made her whimper and moan. The domme was not gentle or slow, riding the submissive she'd been loaned hard and fast, and making her gasp and mumble with excitement.

"Come hard for me, slut. Come now or I swear I will spank you so hard that you won't be able to sit down for a week!" Mistress Chevalier demanded it. "Don't fight it, girl. Come for me, Amber!"

This time, Amber did as she was told. Giving in to the insistent urging in her loins, the need the strapon created in her to climax. She cried out as Mistress Chevalier rode her hard, collapsing into the rug as her orgasm washed over her.

Amber was still gasping, trying to recover her breath when Mistress Chevalier stood up, grabbed her by the hair and hauled her around, forcing the thick length back into her mouth. She sucked and licked at it, putting on a show of cleaning the fake cock for her Mistress.

"Good girl," Mistress Chevalier said when she'd had had her fill of making Amber do that. With a speed which spoke of practice, the domme unbuckled the strapon harness and sat down in a Queen Anne armchair. Amber was impressed when the older woman lifted her legs, and draped them over the high arms of the chair, spreading her legs wide and displaying her pussy.

Sensing that Amber was impressed, "Yoga and years of horse

riding. They're a great combination for improving flexibility. Eat me, slut." The domme laughed and pointed at her glistening pussy with an exaggerated motion.

Amber dove right in, her face already wet with saliva from fellating the silicone cock that lay discarded on the floor. Mistress Chevalier tasted delicious, and she devoured her hungrily.

Soon the domme was sighing and taking deep, contented breaths. "It's hard to believe that you're so new to this. Susanna and her girls are clearly doing an excellent job training you. My compliments on your tongue, girl."

When Amber, too busy to speak her reply, lifted a hand and gave Mistress Chevalier a big thumbs up, the older woman laughed heartily and reached out to cup her head. The domme mashed her sub's face into her pussy as she licked, gently rolling her hips too and grinding herself against the younger woman's face.

"Oh yes, an excellent job indeed," she repeated.

"I'm glad to hear it," Mistress Susanna said.

CHAPTER 8

"Has she made you come, yet?" Mistress Susanna asked.

"Not yet."

"Really? You've been beavering away in here for quite some time. Amber, I must say I'm disappointed with you," Susanna said from somewhere behind her kneeling sub.

Amber's eyes lifted, and she could see Mistress Chevalier's amused smirk as she twisted the situation. She tried to lift her head to explain the situation. That she had only been giving her Mistress's friend head for a few minutes, and the rest of the time she'd been helping set up the stall and getting tormented herself.

Clearly, that wasn't on the card because Mistress Chevalier clamped her thighs together and tightened her grip on Amber's hair, keeping her face firmly pressed against her hungry pussy.

"She seems to be doing her best, but I clearly haven't been able to impress my need on her in the right way," Mistress Chevalier remarked, sounding rather bored with the efforts Amber was making to make her climax, which were entirely earnest.

"Perhaps I could help encourage her for you? I came in to find out what all the noise was about, expecting you to be half-unconscious from her ministrations."

"Oh no, that was Amber, not me. I thought a little reward might help focus her mind. Sadly her tongue, while agile doesn't seem quite dedicated enough," Mistress Chevalier said, winking at Amber.

"I wonder what might do the trick?" Susanna replied.

"There are plenty of great things to try on that table," her friend said.

"Oh, yes, there certainly are. I sense a sales pitch. What beautiful paddles," Susanna said excitedly.

"I do my best," Mistress Chevalier said, smiling down at Amber, who was also doing her best to make the woman come in the hope she might get out of what was about to happen.

"I'm spoilt for choice. Perhaps this nice looking tawse? Or a bamboo paddle?"

"Amber told me that you haven't tried her out as a pony yet," Mistress Chevalier prompted.

"No, not yet. I've thought about it, but there's only so much time in the day, and Amber is so new to the lifestyle. She has a lot to learn, although I honestly thought she was better with her tongue by now," Susann said. She sounded genuinely disappointed, and Amber couldn't help but feel hurt. What Mistress Chevalier was doing was so cruel. She was making Susanna doubt her commitment to serving her Mistress. Making her think her sub wasn't performing well enough and all the while, she was smirking and gloating as Amber's heart was torn in two by the doubt of her Mistress.

"If you'd like to introduce her to some elements of pony play, you could try that horsehair flogger there. The one with the green handle," Mistress Chevalier suggested.

"An excellent choice, the handle is charming, though I'm not sure the colour is ideal," Susanna commented, as she leaned down and pulled Amber's hips back, thus forcing her to all fours. Mistress Chevalier slid down the cushion to a more horizontal position, so Amber wasn't freed from her pussy.

"It's a novel style, popular with youngsters. I can't tell you how many young punks, Goths and anime fans have seen my toys in that vein and offered themselves up to," Mistress Chevalier bragged. "I can do it in any colour of course, but that one does glow in the dark."

Susanna laughed, and the stinging explosion of pain on Amber's buttocks made her scream into Mistress Chevalier's pussy.

"She doesn't like that, does she?" Mistress Chevalier said, gleefully.

"No, but Amber loves to suffer for me, don't you, my dear?" Amber breathed hard through her nose but was finally able to lift her hand and give another thumbs up.

"See? She can take her punishment so well, Jade." Mistress Susanna said.

"That's always good news," Mistress Chevalier said. "I find I have to be very careful using that style of flogger on the university students I meet at conventions. They act like their women of the world and claim to be up for it, but not many have been properly broken in by an experienced domme."

"So, true," Susanna agreed as she delivered two more swishes of the stingy flogger. Amber felt tears well up.

"Keep going, you're making her eyes water," Mistress Chevalier encouraged.

"Of course," Susanna said, delivering more discipline. "Would you like to see her really cry?"

"Tempting but I'd prefer to see you take her to the edge, and maybe one day you'll let me enjoy her tears at my hand?"

"Of course, I'm sure I can complete her punishment without taking her over the line," Susann said, delivering the next few blows at less speed. They still stung, but Amber didn't have to fight the welling up of tears, she could master her reaction to the pain better. "Did you fuck her with this strapon?"

"Yes, she loved it. In her pussy and her mouth too."

"I'm glad she's doing something right. There, all done, Amber," Susanna said, dropping to her knees and using her tongue to soothe Amber's bottom.

"My oh my, Susana. That is hotter than you can imagine," Mistress Chevalier said.

Susanna crawled forward and watched Amber's efforts as she licked at the sopping wet pussy before her. Finally, with Susanna looking on, Mistress Chevalier came hard, shuddering and crying out. Her hands let go of Amber's head and flew to her face. Amber could see her biting her knuckle with excitement as she rode the wave of her orgasm.

Before Amber could speak, Mistress Susanna gripped her head and pulled her into a sloppy and passionate kiss, claiming her mouth with her tongue. Amber was left gasping and flushed.

"That wasn't a bad finish," Mistress Chevalier said.

"She's lying, Mistress!" Amber blurted out. "I'd barely started eating Mistress Chevalier's pussy before you came in. She took her pleasure from me by tormenting my nipples and pussy and making me come, then she fucked me with that thing. I didn't let you down. I was trying really hard to please her. I would never want to disappoint you like that." The two dommes let her rant until she ran out of words and then exchanged a look, before Mistress Chevalier laughed at her, while Susanna passionately kissed her again, on the lips and then all over her face, her hands teasing Amber's breasts.

"You silly girl, of course, you haven't disappointed me. It was just a game we were playing for our pleasure. I'm sorry sweetheart, I thought you knew we were roleplaying," Susanna finally managed to say, looking a little contrite, but not nearly enough for Amber's mood.

"Mistress Chevalier, how did you find my Amber's skills as a cunnilinguist?"

"Top notch, Mistress Susanna. I'd be happy to have her give me head any day of the week, and sixteen times on Sunday," Mistress Chevalier said seriously.

"Sixteen? Only sixteen?" Mistress Susanna teased.

Mistress Chevalier threw her hands up in the air grumpily and then began to pull up her jodhpurs. "Yes, Sundays are usually when I'm at some craft fair or fetish event, marketing my goods. I only have time for half the number of orgasms I usually demand," she said, heaping on the overly theatrical performance like an actor on a television soap.

Mistress Susanna stared blankly at her for a moment, and then both dommes collapsed in a fit of giggles. "Sixteen times!" Mistress Susanna managed, gasping for breath. "Dear me, I can barely breathe."

Amber sat back on her haunches and crossed her arms grumpily, a dark frown taking over her face.

Mistress Chevalier laughed. "Oh no, the subby looks pissed off, Susanna. You're going to pay for this later!" she laughed.

"I'm sure she'll get over it, won't you, my sweetness?" Susanna said. Amber didn't answer.

"Did you enjoy Vicky?"

"Oh yes, she's delightful and so strong," Susanna said.

"Isn't she though? Honestly, I have daydreamed about collaring her," Mistress Chevalier stage whispered conspiratorially.

"I can't say as I blame you, and that does seem to be going around. Yolanda announced earlier she's thinking of collaring Zoe you know," Susanna said.

"Great. Maybe we could have a group ceremony," Mistress Chevalier said. "If you have anyone to collar, we could make it a group thing, perhaps?"

Susanna smiled, "Perhaps, and even if we don't, you should give serious consideration to collaring Vicky before she loses faith that you will. I don't think you'll be happy if that tongue of hers is stolen away by some more giving doom. But for now, we have plenty of fun to have today. I was wondering if you'd like to go and visit Ginger and Pepper, Jade?"

"Are they in your stables? I've never seen your stables you know, I've just met Ginger and Pepper in the grounds or at events you brought them to," Mistress Chevalier pointed out.

"Yes. I thought you might like to see my modest facilities, Amber can take you over to see them. Then when you've said hello, you could bring them back to the party, and we can have them serve drinks. How does that sound?" Susanna suggested.

"Aren't you taking Amber back now?" Mistress Chevalier asked with evident surprise.

"No, I think you should use her for the afternoon at least if you're enjoying her. If you'd like to play with Ginger and Pepper before bringing them in, please feel free to, but if you can keep it fairly short, I'd appreciate it. We want you back at the party with us so we can all have fun together," Mistress Susanna said.

"That's lovely, thank you so much. Amber is a delight to play with. I think we should probably get your ponies in quickly though, so we can join in the fun," Mistress Chevalier said.

"We should have another pony play day soon. Then we can concentrate on your favourite things," Susanna said.

"That would be fun. Perhaps you could even try racing Amber?"

"Maybe. I'm not sure if she is pony material."

"She did rather warm to that horsehair flogger," Mistress Chevalier pointed out.

"True. Perhaps a discussion for another day though. I'll leave you to it. Amber, be good for Mistress Chevalier," Susanna cautioned.

"Yes, Mistress."

CHAPTER 9

"Can I see the rest?" Mistress Chevalier asked as Pepper used her lips to pick up sugar cubes from her outstretched hand and munch the sweet brown sugar down happily.

"The rest? There's really just the tack and playroom, the showers, the stalls and the apartment upstairs where Ginger and Pepper sleep. I think you've seen everything," Amber replied.

"Are you sure? Do you think we have time?"

Amber shrugged. "Mistress wanted me to keep you happy. I'll follow your lead, Mistress Chevalier. We haven't been that long though."

"Good. Let's have a look at the other stalls then," Mistress Chevalier said.

Amber followed as the domme inspected the stalls down from Pepper and Ginger. There were four more in this part of the stable, and only one was in the same good condition as the stalls that Pepper and Ginger played their roles in when called upon.

The other three had seen better days and would need renovation before they'd be appealing to play in. The doors had been cleaned up a bit so that as you approached Pepper's stall, they looked well maintained, but it was just a facade.

"I knew Susanna had done some of the work, but I didn't realise how dilapidated the place was before she bought it. Do you know what's through here?" she asked, heading toward the door at the end of the row of stalls.

"No, I haven't spent much time here outside of the main house. I suppose we could ask Pepper and Ginger, but I think they don't like to break character," Amber said.

The door opened into a much larger stable area, but it was full of muck and cobwebs and clearly hadn't been refurbished at all.

"That's about right, pony and pet play works best if you can keep it up for a while. I don't know anyone who bothers trying to do it 24x7, but with a party going on, it wouldn't be kind to ask them to talk about renovations," Mistress Chevalier agreed. "Look at all this space. There are twelve stalls in this room, and a floor above us."

"I think there are two floors above us, thinking about the windows you can see outside."

"Gosh. I still can't believe how well Susanna has done for herself. She's worked hard as long as I've known here, but some of her businesses really took off. Of course, she got this place for a song at the time. The major cost was all the renovation. I wonder if she's going to renovate more of this?"

"I don't know, Mistress. Mistress Susanna hasn't mentioned anything, but I haven't known her that long."

"It makes my workshop and little paddock seem pitiful by comparison. I really must get a bit more serious about my business. I could never afford something like this, but a little stable and extending my workshop would be lovely," Mistress Chevalier mused.

"Maybe Mistress Susanna could help you find investors or help you market your goods?" Amber suggested.

"That's a kind thought, but she's already letting me bring my wares here so I can try and drum up more business. I'm not sure what I could do with investment anyway. If I had a bigger workshop and more storage, it'd help me be a little more efficient. Even so, there's still a limit to how many harnesses or what have you, that I can make, you see?" Mistress Chevalier explained.

"Perhaps you could get to the point where you could employ some help? You could train someone up to do the basic work for you, maybe?" Amber said.

"That would be nice. Ponyplay is a bit of a niche market, but lots more people are playing with leather goods these days. Maybe I could do more things like paddles and floggers," Mistress Chevalier said.

Amber nodded enthusiastically, "See? Maybe Mistress Susanna would be able to give some better suggestions? I don't know much about business, but she does."

"I can tell you really like helping people, don't you?"

Amber nodded, "I suppose I have. You seem nice, and if you could reach more customers, you'd be in a lot better positions.

"That sounds nice. I do like being in a superior position," Mistress Chevalier replied with a big wink.

"I noticed that," Amber giggled. "It seems to be a lot more popular than I'd have guessed before I applied for my job. I didn't realise so many women liked this stuff."

"Not as many as I'd like but almost enough. I bet you didn't know what you were in for at all, did you?" Mistress Chevalier grinned.

"Being stripped naked, spanked and taught to lick pussy?"

"Yes, it sounds like all that came as something as a surprise. Don't worry, not everyone realises that they are into BDSM without a little push. It's nothing to be embarrassed about," Mistress Chevalier said. "Susanna is very lucky to be able to employ such exciting ladies."

"That's another reason to kick your business into a new gear," Amber pointed out. "You could have a little team of your own too. You could start with one of those girls who like your toys. A little anime fan, maybe?"

"Maybe. Or a cosplay girl who makes her own costumes? That way you could find someone whose crafty like you?"

"I do like being crafty," Mistress Chevalier said. "It would be nice to have another girl at my beck and call. Vicky isn't available all the time, she has a job to go to."

"If I can do anything to help you, do let me know," Amber said.

"One or two things do come to mind, but perhaps we should rejoin the party?"

Amber giggled again. "Yes, probably, but that's up to you, not me. You're the Mistress," Amber teased.

"Oh dear, I'm in charge, aren't I? What a pity," Mistress Chevalier said. Quick as a flash, she closed the distance, and span Amber around, pushing her up against the door of one of the stalls. "You're wet again, aren't you, Amber?" she asked, her breath hot against Amber's ear.

"Yes, Mistress," Amber confessed, as Mistress Chevalier's left hand stroked her breast and her right plunged between her legs.

"You'd like it if I played with this hot little pussy now, wouldn't you?"

"Yes, Mistress. Please," Amber begged.

Mistress Chevalier's strong fingers plunged between her lips and into her pussy, her thumb grazing Amber's swollen clit. "You love that, don't you, slut?"

"Yes, Mistress."

"You girls are all the same, with your eager, tight little pussies. You love having someone take control of you. Having someone teach you how to behave. You'd be on our knees all the time, worshipping my pussy, if you could, wouldn't you?"

Amber nodded and mumbled, "Yes, Mistress." Her body responded to the expert caresses from the domme.

"I know you would dear," Mistress Chevalier agreed, pulling her hands back and leading Amber out to where Pepper and Ginger were waiting. "Now, let's finish getting the ponies ready and get inside shall we?"

"Yes, Mistress," Amber said, the disappointment evident in her voice.

"Awww don't be glum, chum. I promise once we're inside, I'll make good use of you if your Mistress allows it. You'll get what you need."

"You promise? Really?" Amber said with rising excitement.

"I think you and I are going to be good friends, Amber," Mistress

Chevalier said. "I promise to use your hot, young body to put on a great show for everyone. I swear it on my riding crop!"

"Well, that does sound like a cast-iron promise," Amber said with a grin.

"From me? You can take that to the bank."

CHAPTER 10

The ballroom was a riot of imagery that seared itself into Amber's brain for weeks to come. Everywhere she looked, young women were submitting to the dommes that Mistress Susanna had invited.

Mistress Chevalier hugged her from behind, her fingers roving over Amber's body possessively and her mouth hot against her neck as they surveyed the room from the doorway.

"Let's take a tour, shall we, sexy?" Mistress Chevalier asked, nibbling at her ear. They began to walk around through the exhibition of debauchery, voyeuristically appreciating each scene, stopping to watch some and slowing to a stroll for others.

One of the first things they saw was Dame Cartwright and Baroness Carruthers enjoying a display of hand to hand combat.

Holly and Ivy had put their schoolgirl uniforms to one side, and they were wrestling, naked in and covered in shiny oil in the paddling pool. They struggled to remain on top of each other, slipping and sliding around. One would appear to have the upper hand, then would lose her stance and fall to her side with a shriek of laughter.

Each time one of the girls laughed, Dame Cartwright would flick out a long bamboo school cane, lashing their buttocks and making them howl as she admonished them for not taking it seriously. They watched a few tumbles and then Holly planted her sex on Ivy's face and sat on it until Ivy tapped out.

"Make her come then, Ivy," Dame Cartwright ordered, her hand slipping into her tight black skirt and down between her legs as she watched. "You can begin round three after you're done."

Baroness Carruthers had applauded when Holly scored her point and licked her lips lasciviously as she caught sight of her friend masturbating. Slowly, she turned back to face the two subs she had been playing with. Both were now naked and covered in baby oil. Amber wondered if they'd started in the paddling pool.

The Baroness had apparently taken charge of Vicky for the time being, and Mistress Chevalier's well-muscled submissive was sat on the wrestling mats, with her legs wrapped around Charlotte's upper back, ankles crossed and holding her in place. Vicky was holding Charlotte's head with both hands, keeping it tightly pressed to her pussy as the Baroness's submissive serviced her.

"I guess that means Vicky won," Amber said with a giggle.

"Vicky is very tasty, perhaps Charlotte won?" Mistress Chevalier suggested. "Look at the treatment she's getting from her Mistress," Mistress Chevalier said, walking Amber to the side for a better view.

The Baroness had a hand, slick with glistening lubricant, almost to the knuckles on all five digits. Amber gasped and whispered in Mistress Chevalier's ear, "Is she going to?"

Mistress Chevalier gave her an appraising look, then nibbled at her ear, "Is she going to go deeper? Why don't you get down closer for a proper look?"

With that, Mistress Chevalier reached down and gave Amber a fierce, stinging smack across the back of her thighs, causing her to wince in pain and her knees to buckle as the domme expertly dropped her to the floor. She was in control of Amber's descent and by the time she was done, Amber was on her knees near, Charlotte's broad bottom, bent forward, with her hair roughly gripped by Mistress Chevalier's strong fingers.

The scent of Charlotte's arousal was heady, and the slick

squelching noises that Baroness Carruthers fingers made as they withdrew and then pushed back in, were bordering on the obscene. Charlotte was making happy moans as she licked at Vicky, who added to the noise with delighted animalistic noises.

"Have you ever seen this done, Amber?" the Baroness asked.

"No, Baroness," Amber replied, entranced by the way the woman's fingers spread Charlotte's pink lips open.

"Watch closely then," the Baroness demanded as she concentrated on edging her fingers deeper and deeper inside her sub. Charlotte must have been extremely excited because it didn't take much longer until the knuckles passed the threshold of her lips, and the Baroness's hand was swallowed to the wrist.

"Beautiful, isn't it?" Mistress Chevalier said.

"Yes, Mistress," Amber replied as Charlotte began to come and the Baroness's eyes flashed in triumph.

As she was hauled to her feet by the hair, Mistress Chevalier remarked, "I'll remember to tell Susanna how much you admired it, so she can arrange for the Baroness to fist you too, you little slut."

Then they were off again, to see what else was happening. Mistress Chevalier and Amber passed the pirate queen as she flogged one of her serving wenches, who was strapped to a St Andrews Cross. The second wench she'd brought with her was crouched between her widespread legs, eating her pussy as she fondled her own breast and fingered herself.

The cat lady, as Amber had mentally tagged her, was reclining on a chaise longue and enjoying having one kitten worship her feet, as the other put her tongue to use between her legs. The dominant woman opened heavy-lidded eyes as they paused to watch and favoured Amber with a greatly exaggerated wink.

"I think she likes you, Amber," Mistress Chevalier chortled as she pulled the submissive on to the next show.

Mistress Cauldwell was playing with her own submissive, Diamond, who was strapped down to an adjustable spanking bench, her latex panties and bra discarded. The stockings and suspenders were still in place. Diamond was struggling to make her cries of anguish heard past the large ball gag that had been tightly strapped around her mouth.

The cause of her distress was the long, black paddle-like implement which Mistress Cauldwell was slapping against her exposed sex. Her mons Venus was hot pink already, contrasting with the tanned skin of a careful sunbather.

Diamond's legs were strapped to thigh pads and spread as wide as possible, to expose her sex in the most humiliating and vulnerable way imaginable. The bench was curved upward, forcing Diamond's back to arch, and leaving her head lower than her body. It looked uncomfortable in more ways than one.

Amber was fascinated by the way the thick length of leather would impact poor Diamond's prominent mound and then curl down to slap against her labia with a wet smack. Diamond was thrashing against the straps, but her obvious state of arousal betrayed how much she was enjoying the harsh treatment.

"My compliments, Megan," Mistress Chevalier said, "you've created a thoroughly delightful scene."

"Thank you, Jade," Mistress Cauldwell replied. "What do you think of it, Amber? Does our little session delight you as well?"

Amber swallowed hard, "It's quite, umm, intense, Mistress Cauldwell. Is Diamond enjoying it?"

"I believe she is, in the relevant sense anyway. Feel free to touch her and find out," the domme offered generously.

Amber was hesitant to get involved, but Mistress Chevalier stopped holding her hand, and instead, took hold of Ambers left hand with her right, lifting it up and resting it on Diamond's breast. "Feel her nipple. Can you see how stiff it is, how she reacts to your touch?" Mistress Chevalier asked.

"Yes, Mistress. Diamond's nipple feels like it's made of the stuff," she gasped.

"That might convince some people Diamond is enjoying it, but your sub is welcome to taste her pussy, if she still has any qualms," Mistress Cauldwell suggested.

"Are you still concerned about Diamond's pleasure, Amber?"

Mistress Chevalier asked. Amber looked at the two mistresses and hoped she understood the game.

"Yes, Mistress," she replied.

A moment later and Mistress Chevalier was pressing Amber's face hard into Diamond's swollen, sopping lips. "Get your tongue in there, make sure you taste every inch so you can be sure she's turned on, you dirty little slut!" Mistress Chevalier ordered.

Amber could see the length Diamond's body as she licked and sucked at the hot, swollen flesh, and she made eye contact with Mistress Cauldwell who was watching her as if she were a piece of indulgent chocolate cake she was planning to eat.

With growing excitement, Mistress Cauldwell was admiring Amber's pussy eating skills, as she demonstrated them on the tormented submissive's aching pussy. The domme put down her leather strap, hanging it from a hook screwed into the bench, before using both hands to slowly hitch her figure-hugging latex skirt up and over her shapely thighs, until her pussy was exposed too.

As her hands travelled up her body, freeing her admirably large bosom from constraints, Amber got to see the glint of metal in the cleft between her legs as she mounted Diamond's face and demanded her satisfaction. Mistress Cauldwell's slender, tanned fingers found her own pierce nipples and began to play with them.

When Mistress Cauldwell beckoned to Mistress Chevalier, she came forward with excitement, and began to tongue and suck at one of those big perky nipples, like a calf hungry for milk. Mistress Cauldwell let out a contented sigh as she began to ride her submissive's face to orgasm.

Amber did her best to get Diamond there as well and was pleased to see a flash of fire in Mistress's Cauldwell's eyes as her submissive screamed her passion into her pussy, even as she tried to bring her Mistress off.

When the sun-worshipping lovers had had their fill, the two dommes kissed for a while, before Mistress Chevalier said farewell and pulled Amber away, her mouth still wet with Diamond's juices.

When Amber went to wipe it away, the domme forbade it and told her to stay messy for now. Amber blushed profusely at the mere thought of it and was sure the skin of her chest and neck would burn to a crisp from the embarrassment by the time they encountered their next stop on the tour of the ballroom.

Pudding was kneeling beside the exquisite bottom of Jasmine, giving her a thorough spanking. The cook was in a corset and elegant elbow-length gloves, as well as thigh-length books. If Amber hadn't known she was submissive to Mistress Susanna, she would have thought her every bit the dominant.

Jasmine, still in her strappy bondage harness, was on all fours because her face was buried in the pussy of her domme, Mistress Steele. Despite the attentions of her submissive, the domme looked more excited by the pain Pudding was gleefully inflicting on the girl.

"Don't spare the horses, Pudding," Mistress Steel exhorted with a hungry look on her face, as her hand kept Jasmine's head firmly secured against her.

"Yes, Mistress," Pudding agreed.

Mistress Chevalier fondled Amber's backside, even dipping her fingers lightly into the cleft of her buttocks but ultimately, moved them on from the scenario without comment or interrupting the players.

They passed by a few dommes whose names Amber hadn't recalled, playing with subs who were locked in the two big cages. One was on all fours in the coffee table cage, a big vibrator stuffed obscenely in her pussy and a dildo in her mouth that was held to the floor of the cage with a suction cup. The sub was sucking on it obscenely as the dommes around her made lewd comments and reached in to tease her flesh with cruel pinches and slaps.

The sub in the standing cage wasn't faring much better. Although the submissive was standing, she was also manacled by wrist and ankle, spreadeagled and tightly bound. Another sub was crammed in the cage at her feet, teasing her with a powerful sounding wand-style vibrator. The dommes commanding them were threatening the standing sub with terrible punishments if she came without permission.

Mistress Chevalier smiled but swiftly moved them on to where Mistress Yolanda was conducting a session with her sub, Zoe. The sex swing was getting a good test of its stability and strength with this pair. Yolanda was slow-fucking Zoe with a strapon, much to the freshly pierced subs delight.

"Isn't this party marvellous, Yoland?" Mistress Chevalier asked.

Mistress Yoland didn't stop thrusting into her young sub, "It's fantastic. Zoe is beyond excited, aren't you sexy?"

"Fuck, yes! Fuck me harder, Mistress," Zoe begged.

"You're welcome to join us if you'd like?" Mistress Yoland offered generously, "Maybe Amber would like a close-up of Zoe's hood piercing?"

"I think that would be eye-opening for her, but I'm rather keen to give her a thorough workout myself," Mistress Chevalier said. "I'm so horny after seeing all this."

"I know what you mean, this has to be the best party that Susanna has organised yet," Mistress Yolanda agreed. "I'm sure we can play another time. Maybe you and I could have fun while we watch Zoe and Amber?"

"That's definitely something I'm up for if Susanna will lend me Amber, or if you'd like to play with Vicky."

"Maybe you and Vicky and Susanna and Amber should come and try out my new play space one day, I'd love to have some guests," Yolanda suggested.

"Sounds fab, we'll sort something out soon, I promise," Mistress Chevalier said as they left the gothic beauty fucking her nubile submissive with wild abandon.

"So, are you enjoying your first lesbian orgy?" Mistress Chevalier asked.

"Yes, Mistress. Very much. Is it always like this?" Amber asked.

"Not always quite as impressive or in such nice surroundings, but I've been to a lot of exciting events in a similar vein. There are always lots of pretty young women, like yourself, who want to learn about pleasure and pain from old girls like me," Mistress Chevalier said.

"It sounds like you've had a wonderful life, Mistress," Amber said enviously.

"There have been some good times, this is certainly one of them. I've had my share of troubles, but the future is bright, especially for the younger generation. Honestly, it wasn't my generation that had to fight for the most important rights either but I do envy you young things your freedoms," Mistress Chevalier said.

"Oh, is that why you like restricting them so much?" Amber joked.

"It may have been," Mistress Chevalier replied with a knowing wink, "All joking aside, I don't actually know what got me into this, more's the pity. We could talk about that all night, and still not agree on a reason for it. I do know I have lots of thoroughly pleasurable tricks to use on a willing victim like you."

"That sounds fun," Amber said.

"Would you like me to show you some of my tricks now?" Mistress Chevalier asked, pulling Amber in close and kissing her neck, before nibbling at her ear. Her hands roved all over Amber's body as she continued to kiss her deeply. It was a while before they came up for air, and Amber felt too breathless to respond at first.

"Yes, please, Mistress," Amber finally replied.

CHAPTER 11

Amber wasn't sure what Mistress Chevalier had planned but knew that she'd recruited Mistress Susanna to her cause. After a few moments of animated whispering between the two excited dominants, the interrogation chair had been moved to the stage for all to see.

Mistress Chevalier had carefully strapped her down to the chair, which used thick, padded-leather ankle and wrist cuffs. The seat had space for Amber's thighs, but large cutouts in strategic places made her surprisingly accessible.

Another strap from the frame that formed the high back of the chair, went around Amber's forehead and prevented her from so much as turning her head. There was no back-rest to the chair, the frame went up in an arch by her shoulders, and peaked where the headrest was. Her back was left entirely exposed, open to any implement that might be used against it.

The addition of a blindfold, and finally even big can style head-phones playing ambient music, left Amber entirely in her own world. It wasn't long before she felt a certain amount of trepidation. Every now and then, Mistress Chevalier would reach out, and roughly pinch her nipple, or slap her thigh.

Or at least, she assumed it was Mistress Chevalier tormenting her. It could have been any of the women present. The buzz of a vibrator against her trembling knee, made Amber think she would soon receive pleasure as the wielder would slowly drag it up her leg until it was pressed between her thighs.

That wasn't what happened though. Sensation returned in the form of a sharp stinging across Amber's back, from some kind of whip. Amber couldn't hear herself properly over the music from headphones which were doubtless noise-cancelling for extra solitude. She was sure she screamed at the sudden pain though.

A soft dry tongue was placed against her pussy then. It was not a human tongue, Amber realised, from the lack of moisture or wriggling movement, but a tongue of leather. Softly it tapped against her lips, not hard enough to hurt, but slowly and teasingly.

Amber's imagination filled in the rest. One of the dommes was going to give her the pussy spanking she probably deserved for being such a slut. It would be agonising and they would laugh and delight in her suffering.

Fingers danced the length of the cleft between her cheeks, and then two pairs of hands helped spread her buttocks apart. She wondered which of the many women present was holding her wide like that, to reveal her puckered hole.

When the fingers returned, they were damp with lubricant and began to work themselves deep inside her. Amber felt shame as she realised there was little resistance to the intrusion, not because she was gaping open unnaturally, but because she was surprisingly relaxed in her state of arousal. Her sphincter wasn't tight with anxiety but allowed the slowly thrusting digits to coat her with thick, cool, jelly.

A broad-based butt plug, which Amber imagined to be the largest she had yet received, was pushed slowly, ever so slowly, into her welcoming arse. Then it was jiggled, and tugged, pushed a little deeper, as the dommes tested it's fit. Amber could feel the excitement, leaving a thin trail of liquid down her thighs. She imagined the excited onlookers pointing at the juices dripping from her pussy and commenting on how much of a slut she was.

For a while, a long rubber bit gag was forced into her mouth, and it pulled her cheeks back uncomfortably, considerably lessening her ability to cry out. That was right after both her nipples were pinched quite fiercely and she screamed again.

The pain was intense, and she thrashed against the chair while it subsided to the point she could control her response. The pressure remained, and then Amber realised a weight hung from her nipples, a length of cold metal draped over her torso. It had to be a set of clamps and a chain between them.

Soft kisses made a bizarre counterpoint to her suffering. There was a flurry of them, against her inner thighs, down her spine, on her feet, her face, and breasts. Where there was exposed flesh, soft, warm lips were pressed against her and tongues were lightly brought into play.

Amber was left alone for a while, and all she could feel was the faintest breeze of people moving around her, and the shaking of the stage as people moved across it. She could no longer picture what might be going on. Who was helping with her torment? The kisses had come from at least four people at once, and it could easily have been more. Were mistresses still fucking their subs as they watched the performance with vague interest?

Or were they all sitting quietly, completely engrossed in the events on the stage? The thought of being watched like that didn't temper Amber's arousal, but rather inflame it.

Her need to have something dramatic happen, whether it be pleasurable or painful, grew with every passing moment until finally her straps were unbuckled.

Strong hands took hold of Amber by her upper arms, helping her to her feet. Whoever it was, supported and guided her, marching her across the stage. Amber was still blindfolded, gagged and had headphones on, she stumbled a little, but they didn't let her fall.

A firm body pressed against her from behind, and her captors held her arms up high. Hands stroked up her sides, and she smelled the nearby scent of baby oil, as the fingers reached her breasts, and danced over the clamps that still tormented them.

Amber knew she was whimpering, though she couldn't be sure if it was from pain, excitement or fear at this point. The hands ended up behind her neck, strong fingers interlaced in a full-nelson that held her tightly in place. Her back pressed against Vicky's surgically enhanced breasts, the woman's nipples were as stiff as bullets. It had to be Vicky, only she was tall, strong and firm enough, combined with the scent of baby oil.

Sound rushed back to her as the headphones were removed. Someone was talking, but she didn't know who.

"Amber Hannam, you have been charged with wanton and slovenly behaviour and in addition, the tempting of good women into your sinful embrace. How do you plead?" an unknown official said.

Amber took a moment to catch up, and the question was repeated. "How do you plead?"

"Not guilty! I have done nothing wrong!" she cried out.

"We have your confession. The entire court heard it when you were in the chair."

"Lies, you tortured me. You can't hold me to anything I said to ease my suffering. I have done nothing wrong, only that which my Mistress ordered," Amber replied, getting into the swing of things and wondering where this would go.

"It is your Mistress who has brought you to this court for judgement, Amber," the voice answered. Amber thought it was most likely Jade, but since the woman was putting on a rather hammy theatrical voice, she couldn't be sure. The key to roleplaying an improvised scenario, she'd once heard an actor say, was to always say yes. Not literally, but to go with the flow of other people's input and dialogue, rather than argue with it.

"No! Why would my Mistress betray me? I have only ever served at her command," Amber wailed with as much hurt as she could manage.

"Do you deny the charges?"

"Yes!"

"You did not attempt to pervert the course of a competition by offering inducements to the ponygirl, Pepper? Inducements of a sexual nature," the interrogator asked.

Amber hung her head, "Yes, I did, but it was only supposed to be fun."

"Was it only supposed to be fun when you wantonly applied your tongue to the task of alleviating the distress that the servant known as Diamond, was experiencing, after receiving a lawful punishment?" the prosecutor asked, concluding, "I warn you, that Mistress Cauldwell has already testified that having used lawful disciplinary measures against Diamond's intimate person, you did everything in your power to turn her against her employer."

"You're twisting what happened. I was ordered to lick Diamond's pussy, for the amusement of her mistress," Amber protested.

"Ladies of the jury, can you see what we have to deal with here?" the prosecutor said. "It seems clear that Amber Hannam is a slut. A wanton temptress who uses her voluptuous, youthful body, to corrupt innocent young women. Her actions have proven that she is so skilled in the arts of seduction, that she can even cause the most respected of women to abandon their good senses."

"Are there more examples the prosecution wishes to give?"

"Certainly M'Lady. Why, only today, I saw Miss Hannam offering her body to several gentlewomen in exchange for favours of a sexual nature."

"Shameless!" someone cried out.

"Ladies, please hand your decision to the bailiff," another voice called out, cutting through the discussion among the jury.

After a heartbeat, the judge solemnly intoned, "Amber Hanna, it is the verdict of this jury that you are guilty of all charges mentioned in court today, and more besides I'll warrant. It is not appropriate for a judge to act as a witness in a trial, but now that the verdict has been handed down I can add my own comments. I witnessed this slut, having enticed a gentlewoman of this town to dally with her, to her own pleasure, refuse to properly worship the Mistress to whom she was assigned. Miss Hannam left her Mistress without relief for some good while, and I had to intercede myself, disciplining her with a flogger until she fulfilled one of the few duties her tongue is useful for."

The judge waited while the court returned to quiet after this terrible secret was revealed. It seemed to Amber that this wasn't all above board as trials went, but perhaps it was a fair cop. She could hardly completely deny all the instances that they might bring up.

"Your honour," she spoke up, "I confess. I'm guilty. Of all these things and more. Please, have mercy on my poor body. I don't want to be transported to Australia. I beg you, your honour. I will take any punishment you deem suitable to atone for my behaviour."

"Silence in court!" the bailiff holding Amber tightly called out.

"It is too late for you to earn favour through confession, Amber Hannam. You stand condemned as a wanton slut, a young woman who tempts and teases, offering herself up to all and sundry for her own gain. You are a succubus in the midst of our community, and I fear if we do not deal with you harshly, you will continue to disrupt our lives. You will be placed in the pillory, until such time as I see fit to release you, there to serve your sentence with your body. You will pay for your crime, with the same body with which you have committed it and may the women of the town have mercy on your flesh, for I assure you, I will not," the judge said before banging the gavel.

Two people took her arms again, and the wrestling hold was released. Vicky and the other two women positioned Amber and then removed her blindfold. Blinking furiously as her eyes filled with tears from the sudden light, Amber was finally able to make out the room.

Mistress Susanna was seated on one of the Queen Anne high backed armchairs that had been brought on stage so that she could act as the judge. Mistress Chevalier had been her prosecutor and now advanced on the shivering nude submissive, to carry out her punishment.

Amber was forced into the pillory. Her wrists and neck were placed in the bottom curve of the cutouts the pillory had for them, then measured. Some additional sections were latched in place, to bring the large holes down to the correct size for her neck and wrists. A useful innovation that no doubt a lot of people would have been thrilled to see when the town's still punished people like this. Then the clamp was closed over her neck and wrists. Mistress Chevalier slipped fingers between her skin and the padding to check the fit and nodded with satisfaction.

For a moment, Amber worried they might actually throw rotten fruit at her and had to bite her lip hard to stop from laughing, which she didn't think would be smart at this juncture.

Amber's ankles were swiftly shackled to the floor with heavy metal cuffs, and short chains to hold her feet just where they were wanted. The frame of the pillory had a sliding mechanism, and the height was adjusted to perfectly fit the current occupant.

Sugar lifted Amber's head up by the hair, so she was forced to look in front, where Candy was standing by a table, covered with a cloth. Sugar leaned in, and kissed Amber's neck hungrily before whispering in her ear, "As ordered by the court here are the instruments of your punishment." Sugar waved her hand as Candy drew back the cloth.

"Begin," Susanna ordered, from the chair she lounged in, which was just within view if Amber turned her head to the left and offered an excellent view of both sides of the pillory. "Sugar, Candy, attend me."

There was no time to appreciate the atmosphere or the visuals provided by the audience of women whose submissives were preparing to please them. Mistress Chevalier began without choosing an implement, as Sugar had suggested. The sting of her palm against Amber's tender buttock drew a whimper of pain.

Amber took deep breaths, and steadied her feet, preparing for what was to come, knowing it would become increasingly severe as Mistress Chevalier worked her way along the table. She took the spanking well, keeping the tears from her eyes and managing to control any outbursts.

Roxy stepped forward, leaned down and kissed Amber firmly on the mouth, to general murmurs and comments of approval. Then she straightened up, smiling wickedly at the bemused occupant of the pillory and moving to the table of torture, as Amber has begun thinking of it.

The chauffeur drummed her fingers over the table as she the length of it, touching each tool briefly and glancing back at Amber as if trying to make a decision about which implement to choose. Finally, she selected one and passed it over the pillory to Mistress Chevalier. The paddle brought Amber to the next level of resistance, she scrunched her toes, bit her lip, tried to find her happy place, anything and everything to avoid crying out.

When Roxy put it back on the table and picked out a riding crop, which was soon put to good use on Amber's inner thighs. The swishing blows were not as hard as she'd been spanked and paddled, but they didn't need to be. The sensitive skin of her thighs produced stinging sensations that Amber couldn't ignore.

"Barely a whimper from this one, ladies," Mistress Chevalier remarked. "What a trooper she is, eh? Mistress Susanna, you have found yourself a real treasure here."

"I'm so glad you all approve," Mistress Susanna commented, her voice sounding slightly off-kilter. Amber glanced to her side and could see Sugar kissing their Mistress on the neck, and Candy working away between her legs. Mistress Susanna caught her looking and smiled wickedly, blowing her a kiss. "Roxy, why don't you pass Mistress Chevalier that lovely rattan cane?"

This instruction produced gasps of mock horror and filthy laughter from around the room. Amber could tell these women didn't think she could hold out against it. When she saw the cane Roxy had picked up, she had her own doubts. It was long, with a crooked handle and looked quite heavy.

Mistress Chevalier swished it around menacingly and then struck without warning. Amber gritted her teeth and resisted crying out, squeezing her eyes shut as the second swipe landed across her hot bottom. Turning her head, she saw Mistress Susanna smiling at her. Then she mouthed something as the third strike landed.

Again, Mistress Susanna mouthed a sentence and Amber understood this time. When the fourth strike landed, she let forth her response. Her sudden cry of pain silenced the hall for a few seconds before Mistress Chevalier landed her followup, and Amber cried out piteously again. That pleased the audience, and the dominant women watching their friend's new submissive caned so harshly, let out an encouraging cheer.

Amber shot them a reproachful look, but it didn't help. Her suffering merely amused them and hoping that they might be sympathetic to her plight wasn't going to get her anyway.

There was no point holding back any longer, trying to be brave for her Mistress, to impress anyone. As the next two stripes bit into her buttocks, Amber let her tears flow freely, and her voice became a vent for all her pain.

Mistress Chevalier moved to the front of the pillory, and crouched, taking Ambers mouth and covering it with her own, her tongue plunged deep inside the submissive girl and claimed her. Amber responded as if her own Mistress was kissing her and not a proxy with temporary control over her body.

Finally, Mistress Chevalier stood and approached Mistress Susanna, "Your honour," she said, bowing before her with a flourish. "Is Amber's punishment complete, or do you wish to see something else?"

Mistress Susanna stood up, "Thank you, Mistress Chevalier, for such an enjoyable scenario. I think I can speak for all of us when I saw that was most satisfying. I had intended to take Amber back at some point, but I do think you have more than earned the right to continue you using her as you see fit. I only have one request, I would like to see her fucked with the strapon you used earlier in private if you wouldn't mind putting on a bit more of a show."

"Of course. Vicky, fetch my toy and harness me," Mistress Chevalier ordered. It wasn't long before the dommes were crowded around Amber's rear, watching Mistress Chevalier pound the strapon into her aching pussy and enjoying the sound of her lusty moans.

Mistress Susanna gave free permission for the women to touch and toy with her, provided Mistress Chevalier did not object. Amber's body became a plaything for the dommes, as they pinched, spanked, fingered and stroked her. All the while, Mistress Chevalier fucked her powerfully with her favourite strapon.

When the domme's legs began to tire, Amber breathed a sigh of relief. Until the Baroness stepped forward, an oddly bulbous, luminous orange strapon jutting from her thighs.

"May I play?" the Baroness asked.

Dame Cartwright also stepped forward, in her headmistress gear, and holding a long ruler. "I'd like to play too, if I may?"

Mistress Susanna and Mistress Chevalier both gave their blessing, and indeed, Amber heard, strong encouragement to their desires.

Her mouth was soon occupied with the silicone cock of the Baroness, and her breasts became the property of Holly and Ivy, as they fondled them and suckled on her hard nipples. Meanwhile, the Dame used her long ruler to turn a lower section of Amber's bottom scarlet. Dame Cartwright was a firm spanker, counting out her strokes with each swipe.

The Baroness soon tired of her mouth and moved back to fuck Amber's pussy instead. Dame Cartwright moved to the front, ordering Ivy to her knees next to the pillory. The mistress raised her foot and placed it on her sub's shoulder, and due to her height, Amber was able to nuzzle at her pussy, if not do a sterling job.

When they were done with her, Dame Cartwright had not been able to reach a climax but rectified that by laying back on one of the chaises longues. Ivy was tasked with eating her Mistress's well-stimulated pussy, and Holly was given the honour of straddling her face, to be the recipient of her domme's tongue.

Amber thought she'd surely be released then, but the Baroness had other ideas. A footstool was positioned in front of the pillory, and the height of the clamp section was lowered until Amber was forced to drop to all fours. The Baroness presented her pussy for Amber to worship and like the slut everyone expected her to be, she dove in happily.

Mistress Chevalier was not done with her, either, it seemed. She collected several willing dommes and lined them up on a cushion behind Amber. Soon her pussy was being repeatedly claimed by a train of Mistresses, and she lost herself to wave after wave of powerful orgasms, even as her tongue satisfied the Baroness multiple times.

When the dommes finally had their fill of alternating between fucking Amber's pussy and using her mouth to make them come, Mistress Chevalier finally released her and used a damp cloth to clean her up a little.

"I think it's time for me to reclaim my girl, Jade. If that's alright with you?"

"Of course, Mistress Susanna. I should think she needs some rest after such a long day. Amber, thank you for being such a good sport," Mistress Chevalier said.

"Thank you for taking such good care of me, and using me so well, Mistress Chevalier," Amber replied as she melted into a hug with Mistress Susanna.

"You are most welcome, my sexy young friend," Mistress Chevalier replied.

"Thank you, too, Mistress," Amber said, gazing up at Susanna adoringly.

CHAPTER 12

Susanna relaxed with Amber on a large sofa. Mistress Chevalier and her sub, Vicky were entwined on the other end. The maids had fetched them all chilled fruit juice to quench their thirst while they took a break.

Eventually, Susanna looked down at her sub, and made her an offer, "Now, Amber. I feel you are due a reward of some kind for your much-appreciated efforts today. Is there anything you would like?"

Amber pondered the question for a while before cautiously asking, "Is it permitted to ask Mistress Chevalier for something?"

"Certainly, but I shall warn you, if you offend her she'll probably spank you again, and I'll let her."

"Yes, Mistress. Thank you. Mistress Chevalier, would you do me the honour of letting me play with Vicky for a while, so that you and Mistress Susanna can watch us?"

Mistress Chevalier grinned wickedly, "Of course, but I think which of you in charge of this little show, should be decided in the paddling pool, don't you?"

"That's hardly fair, Vicky is sure to win with her muscles," Susanna replied. Then she looked at Vicky hungrily and continued, "I agree. Vicky, please be careful with my sub, you might easily break her. But once you've won, please know that I have no objection to you humiliating her, riding her face, spanking her or anything of the sort. Indeed, I'm sure it would be amusing to watch you demand your pleasure from her, whatever your personal preferences are."

Amber swallowed hard as Vicky turned toward her with a predatory look in her eyes, and politely rumbled her response, "Don't worry, you little slut. You have made my Mistress very happy today, I won't injure you."

"Thank you, that's kind of you, Vicky," Amber said as they wall walked off to the paddling pool and the huge sub grabbed a big bottle of baby oil, and squeezed it all over Amber's body. Vicky leaned down as she began to spread the oil over Amber's body, kissing her hard on the mouth.

Vicky's hands found Amber's breasts and coated them with baby oil as their mistresses took to a nearby sofa to watch. "I won't injure you, Amber. But I'd love to hear you say, 'Cotswold' for me," Vicky said loudly.

Mistress Susanna laughed, "I think Amber may have bitten off more than she can chew, don't you, Mistress Chevalier?"

"I'm sure Vicky will be kind to her."

Amber let forth a startled yelp, as Vicky's powerful fingers clamped down on her nipples with vice-like security, and she tugged her forward. "I won't injure you, but I'm going to make you scream in more ways than one, pretty little slut," Vicky laughed.

Vicky's strong fingers gripped Amber's shoulders and forced her to her knees, clamping her head against her pussy. "Lick me, bitch," she growled.

Amber's nipples were still smarting, and she felt thoroughly chastened by the sudden control that Vicky had gained over her, which wasn't what she'd been hoping for. Her cheeks flushed scarlet with shame as she complied with Vicky's demand and began to tongue her vigorously. Amber's hands found her breasts and massaged the sore nipples briefly, before inexorably sliding down her stomach and between her legs.

Mistress Chevalier noticed that the young submissive had begun to masturbate, as Vicky ground her pussy into her opponents face, and pointed it out to Susanna, who laughed along with her.

For Amber, the evening did not get any less challenging. After each orgasm she gave Vicky, the Amazonian woman would push her back roughly, and Amber would end up sprawled on the other side of the pool thanks to their baby oil coating.

One of their Mistresses would say, "Ding, ding!" as if starting a boxing match, and then Vicky would decide to either win immediately or draw it out, letting Amber see some hope of a victory, only to dash it at the last moment and subjugate the younger and significantly smaller woman.

Vicky heaped humiliation on Amber, bringing her to tears by spanking her over her knee or leaving her coughing and spluttering for air after pinning her to the ground and riding her tongue and lips like a sex toy, or even flipping her upside down and clamping her mouth to Amber's pussy, and licking her to a powerful orgasm.

That last bout wasn't so bad, of course, but it was still embarrassing to be so thoroughly controlled, not through choice, rather through pure physical superiority.

Then Mistress Susanna had an idea and tossed in a positively enormous silicone dildo, that came to rest between the girls before the next match was started. A harness followed.

Vicky looked at the thing and cracked her knuckles, "I'll go easy on you, if you turn around now, and drop to all fours, like a good little slut."

Amber almost did it, almost gave in entirely. But then she saw the look on Vicky's face and dove for the weapon, lifting it triumphantly.

A second later, Vicky's powerful hand was on her neck, and she was face down, arse up in the slippery paddling pool, getting spanked hard for challenging Mistress Chevalier's champion. Vicky made her strap the harness on her, and fit the big cock, then kiss the tip respectfully before coating it with oil.

"Well?" Vicky said, expectantly, when Amber was done.

"It's better to lose with some dignity, Amber," Mistress Susanna chimed in.

Amber swallowed hard and bowed her head. Then she admitted to herself that she had been defeated, and turned around, putting her face back to the lining of the paddling pool, and carefully raising herself up on her knees to get her bottom as high as possible for the big woman.

Vicky's left hand gripped her waist, hard to counter the slippery oil, and her right forefinger pressed firmly against the butt plug that was still in Amber's arse. Amber gasped in surprise and groaned with humiliation when Vicky tugged gently on the butt plug.

"No, please," she begged the victor. "Please don't," Amber whimpered plaintively. Perhaps Vicky would grant her mercy and fuck her aching pussy?

"No mercy!" Mistress Susanna called out, laughing cruelly.

"Oh, you are mean sometimes, Susanna," Mistress Chevalier said sympathetically. Then she too burst out laughing. "Fuck her, Vicky."

Vicky didn't yank the butt plug out, which might have been kinder. Instead, she teased Amber with it, pulling it back until the wide base was almost free, and then shoving it back in and making Amber yelp. The cruel teasing only made her pussy wetter, and her otherwise useless hand found her pussy, plunging fingers inside herself. No-one stopped her, although the filthy comments about her slutty behaviour proved they had noticed.

The butt plug finally came free with a pop, and Amber felt the big head of the cock stretch her even wider, and Vicky pushed it expertly into her arse. Amber cried out as an orgasm ripped through her, and when the slow-motion of Vicky fucking her began to steadily build pace, she could not help but cry out some more.

Amber was thoroughly exhausted by the time Vicky had given up on fucking her, unstrapping the harness from her loins and leaving the silicone monster buried in Amber's aching arse.

Vicky stood up and towered over her. "Ready?"

"Please, Vicky, no more? I beg you," Amber pleaded.

"If you want this to stop, begging won't help," Vicky said, slapping her meaty hand down hard on Amber's backside and making her tear up again. "I won't stop until you tell me what I want to hear."

"What's that?" Amber said, yelping as Vicky brought her hand down again. The big woman kept going for a while, with big meaty slaps that made Amber swear like a sailor.

"You're pushing your arse up to meet me, Amber."

"Am I?" Amber groaned, as innocently as she could manage.

"Yes. You are! You filthy little slut. You'll regret that, if you don't tell me what you know I want to hear," Vicky said, flinging the strapon down by Amber's head for emphasis. Then she delivered a few more spine-tingling smacks for good measure.

"Ok, ok," Amber cried. "Cotswold. Is that what you want?"

Vicky stopped what she was doing. "Better."

Amber was pulled up from the ground and into a warm embrace. Vicky whispered into her ear, "Are you alright, slut?"

Amber whimpered as the big woman hugged her, "Yes. I'll be fine. Thank you, Vicky."

"Good. You used your safeword, so I have to stop. But I'm not really finished with you. Would you like to play some more? I promise I'll be nicer, now I've beaten you," Vicky purred seductively.

Amber was amazed. "You want to keep going."

"Yeah, baby. As long as our Mistresses will let us. Can you take it? What do you say?" Vicky kissed Amber's neck, and she felt herself weakening.

"Yes, I say yes. Do your worst," Amber replied.

"You can always use your safeword again, but I'm not after it this time," Vicky pointed out.

"I hope I won't need it."

Vicky pushed her back to the floor, and Amber squealed in surprise.

"Enough cuddling and sweet talk, slut. Put your mouth where it belongs, and do a good job, then maybe I'll let you go," Vicky offered.

Amber looked up at Vicky from the floor defiantly and said something rude.

Vicky grinned and flung herself at the smaller sub, wrestling her into a prone position. "You'll do as you're told, my girl, or I'll strap that back on, and fuck you twice as hard," Vicky boasted, gesturing to the silicone cock and harness.

Amber went limp, utterly defeated again. The big woman shifted her knees to a new position, and smiled down triumphantly at Amber, looming above her like a conquering Empress. Amber accepted her fate, and Vicky read the submission in her eyes.

Without another word, the victor straddled Amber's head, a knee on either side and began to descend at a frustratingly unhurried speed. Amber watched as the might woman filled her vision.

"Oh boy," was all she could say before her mouth was otherwise occupied for some time.

CHAPTER 13

It was gone three am before Amber finally crawled into bed, and Susanna cuddled up behind her.

"Did you have a good day, Mistress?" she asked.

"Yes, it was wonderful, Amber. Thank you for being such a welcoming host to all my guests," Susanna replied.

They lay like that for a while, and Amber thought she dozed off for a bit, or perhaps she just closed her eyes for a moment. She rolled over to face Susanna and saw her domme was restless too.

"Mistress, I have an idea I wanted to tell you about."

"If it involves me spanking you, or something like it, I'm afraid it'll have to wait until morning," Susanna said, leaning forward and kissing her sub.

"No, it's a business idea. Is it ok if I explain it?"

Susanna smiled. "Certainly, but if I fall asleep while you do, don't take it personally. I haven't been so exhausted in years."

"Well, Mistress Chevalier has a bit of a business problem," Amber began.

"Yes, she doesn't have a great head for it," Susanna agreed.

"Her space is limited, she doesn't have room for a shop on site, and she doesn't even have a stable to use with Vicky," Amber said.

"Don't beat around the bush, go ahead."

"You have a great big stable, but it needs renovating, and you've got other buildings that are vacant too. What if we got the stables spruced up, cleared out some space, and expanded the upstairs flats. Mistress Chevalier could use the stables for her pony, set up a workshop in the outbuildings, and a small shop, and live in a new flat." Amber suggested.

"That sounds great for Mistress Chevalier but expensive for me. What do I get out of it?" Susanna murmured sleepily.

"It wouldn't have to be expensive, we could do as much of the clearing up and basic work as possible ourselves. You pay a big premium having builders do that sort of thing for you when it's unskilled labour."

"What do you know about that?"

"I have friends who worked in building trades," Amber said.

"Right, so renovating more of the buildings wouldn't cost as much if we planned it well. Still, what's the actual upside you see for me? I don't make business decisions without a clear goal," Susanna pointed out gently.

"You would have an expert on pony play on site all the time. Pepper and Ginger would have more people to take care of their needs, and you wouldn't worry about them if you were away. You could get any custom leatherwork done that you wanted, within reason," Amber said.

"I hope that's not it. I'm quite happy with how Pepper and Ginger live and I'm sure I can get my leather needs met without needing to do any building work," Susanna pointed out.

"In addition, Mistress Chevalier would pay you rent and having her shop on the grounds would bring more kinky ladies to visit, which I think you'd enjoy. Your property would be more valuable with another flat, and I'm guessing you have planning permission to renovate it all anyway. You could rent out your stables for ponyplay events too, like a holiday letting for kinky people."

"You're getting warmer. Anything else to interest me?"

"If you had Mistress Chevalier as your Stable Mistress, you could have more ponies. I think you'd like more girls in there, wouldn't you?"

Susanna raised an eyebrow and sat up a bit. "You're encouraging me to split my time with you even more?"

"I think I could still persuade you to spend lots of time with me," Amber said confidently. "Plus, I think you'd enjoy having easy access to Vicky or any other girls Mistress Chevalier knows.

"You seem sure of yourself all of a sudden," Susanna replied. "But you're right, Vicky is appealing, and I would certainly tumble her again if I had the chance.

Amber boldly slipped two fingers inside her Mistress, which soon shifted the discussion. "I am feeling more confident, Mistress. That's your influence. I think you like me enough that you'd want my touch, even if you had a dozen more girls to tend to your needs."

Susanna's hand clamped down over Amber's, and she growled, "Make me come while you explain the rest of your idea, slut and you might have a deal."

So Amber did just that.

CHAPTER 14

"Good morning, Susanna," Mistress Chevalier said. "Thank you for the overnight stay."

"Good morning, Jade. Did you and Vicky enjoy yourselves?" Susanna asked, smiling at the tall, powerful submissive woman that Mistress Chevalier had arrived with.

Vicky was no longer dressed in her ponygirl outfit but in a long, sheer chemise. She was kneeling in front of the sofa on which Mistress Chevalier sat, drinking her tea. The chemise offered tantalising glimpses of her muscular form and large, rounded breasts. Amber had to concentrate hard not to gape at the appealing cleavage that Vicky had on display.

Mistress Chevalier reached out and stroked the back of Vicky's head, causing the submissive woman to tilt her head and assume a dreamlike expression. "Yes, Vicky is wonderfully sore all over. She whimpered a lot this morning when I took her. I loved seeing that you'd all made such good use of her."

"I'm glad to hear you're both happy. Vicky was a very popular girl, yesterday, and such an obedient one too," Susanna commented.

"I get the impression that we aren't in here on our own to talk about how enjoyable Vicky is as a plaything though."

Susanna smiled, "Amber had an idea that she suggested to me. I thought it was quite promising, so I suggested that she be the one to propose it to you."

Mistress Chevalier raised an eyebrow. "Amber had an idea, did she? I'm all ears."

"After we spoke in the stables, I had a much better idea. Well, I thought it might be, and then I talked it over with Mistress this morning, and she agreed."

"I see. This is a business idea, I assume?" Mistress Chevalier said, frowning.

"Yes but let me explain it before you decide," Amber said.

Mistress Chevalier nodded and allowed Amber to go through the ideas. She asked some questions and seemed happy enough with the answers.

"That does sound good. Are you really on board with this, Susanna? My rental term is up in just over two months, and I'd hate to reject signing up again, and for this to fall through."

"Don't worry, I won't leave you high and dry. If you're up for it in principle, I'll have a contract proposal over to you by Tuesday, and you can let me know if you need any amendments. I'll make sure your rental agreement protects us both in the event you take a strong disliking to me," Susanna said.

"I think it's more likely you'd get annoyed with me," Mistress Chevalier said.

"Not at all. I would never treat you badly," Susanna said. "Not even if we had a disagreement over something. You're one of my favourite people. Otherwise, I wouldn't be going along with this investment in the property. Unless your business has a sudden boom, I won't cover my costs of renovating the buildings. It's a good idea to get it done but not urgent. The estate is too big for us, though, so it would be nice to have more people here, and a few more visitors."

"Would it be a problem if Vicky moved in with me?" Mistress Chevalier asked. Vicky gasped, startled by the remark and her head whipped round to stare lovingly at her domme.

"Of course, if we move quickly, we might be able to get a second flat finished before you move in. If not, we do have spare bedrooms in the house you could use. I'm sure Vicky would be very welcome about the estate," Susanna said.

"Wonderful. Now, how do you see the pecking order working? Two dominant women in the same location and you want me to take charge of two of your subs on a day to day basis," Mistress Chevalier said, leaving the thought hanging.

"I recall you saying yesterday that I could bend you over and spank you any time I wanted," Susanna said with a sly smile.

"Would you like that to be our dynamic, then? For me to be your submissive, but dominant to the girls when needed?" Mistress Chevalier asked, calmly sipping her tea while she waited for Susanna to respond.

"You would describe yourself as a switch, would you not, Jade?" Susanna said presently.

"I mostly take the dominant role these days, but I do still enjoy offering my submission to some people. Every now and then," Jade replied.

"Then how about this, we are both dommes, and when it's required, helpful or enjoyable, I will share my girls with you. I will ask them to submit to your pleasure, just as they do to mine. I imagine they will all be comfortable with that arrangement. I will also, from time to time, ask you to submit to me. Generally, you will agree to do so, while I have no intention of submitting to you, or anyone else," Susanna stated.

"I could enjoy that," Mistress Chevalier said. "I would, in turn, offer any sub I had for your use at times, provided they were similarly agreeable. Vicky, would you agree to submit to Mistress Susanna if I asked it of you?"

Vicky was still looking at her Mistress adoringly since she'd suggested that she move in at the stables with her Mistress. She nodded eagerly in reply but did not speak.

"Does that settle it then?"

"Yes, I think we have an agreement in principle."

Mistress Chevalier smiled and replied, "Here's to a beautiful tenancy, kid!" She lifted her tea and chinked her cup against Susanna's to seal the deal. "I'm pretty sure that only works with alcohol, but I'm sure we can cope. Everyone is still here, having breakfast. Would you like to tell them, perhaps?"

"That you're moving into my outbuildings?"

Mistress Chevalier laughed, "No, though that too. I thought you might enjoy telling them that you were going to be in charge of me now and then. I'm sure some of them would love the thought of me being spanked by you."

"They would probably prefer the sight of you being spanked," Susanna pointed out.

Mistress Chevalier exclaimed in a theatrical voice, "But, Mistress Susanna, surely you wouldn't take down my panties and spank me hard in front of all our friends?" Her hand flew to her mouth, covering it in horror at the thought of it.

"Indeed I would, for a woman who deserves a firm spanking should accept that it might need to be carried out under the watchful eye of her peers," Susanna replied. "Amber, please go to the conservatory and ask the ladies taking breakfast to join us in the ballroom. I have important news for them to hear!"

Amber managed to round up all the dommes and their various subs and persuade them to finish up their breakfasts and come to the ballroom to hear what Susanna had to say to them. There was a little grumbling from some who hadn't quite finished their breakfasts, and more when Amber had to refuse to tell them what they were being summoned to hear. It took all her patience not to blurt it out excitedly.

Finally, everyone filed into the ballroom, Amber bringing up the rear to make sure there weren't any stragglers. Susanna was standing on the stage in the centre of the room, with Vicky kneeling next to Mistress Chevalier beside her.

Sugar, Candy, Roxy, Pudding, Pepper and Ginger had all been called to the room to listen as well and were politely standing at the back, behind Mistress Susanna's friends. Amber tiptoed over to stand with them.

"Ladies, I have a little announcement to make in a moment, but first, let me thank you all for coming and making this such a wonderful get together. It's always a pleasure to play host to our little gatherings, and I hope you all enjoyed yourselves as much as I did," Susanna said. The ladies favoured her with a polite round of applause and polite remarks before she went on.

"As you all know, Mistress Chevalier is a fixture in the pony play community, both as an acknowledged pony training expert and as a source of equipment, clothing and tools. What you may not know is that her current workshop premises are somewhat cramped which limits the number and type of projects she can work on at once and excludes the possibility of hiring staff to help run the business," Susann said.

"It's worth the wait though," Baroness Carruthers commented, "the best leather gear I've ever paid good money for."

"I agree. My own girls were wearing Mistress Chevalier's work yesterday. Amber has suggested an idea which we all think will help Mistress Chevalier grow her business, and make my estate much more vibrant in the near future. We will be continuing the development of my stable buildings, adding new flats, at least another dozen stalls for ponies and perhaps most importantly, a workshop and shop space for Mistress Chevalier," Susanna explained.

The audience chatted amongst themselves, excitedly for a few moments before Susanna's calming hand motions quieted them. "Ladies, if I may continue. In addition, Jade will take up a position as my Stable Mistress. We will hold more pony events for those who are interested, and I hope more events like this weekend."

That drew a resounding cheer from all assembled.

"So Mistress Chevalier is going to join your stable of girls, eh, Susanna?" Mistress Yolanda asked.

A few of the dommes chorused, "Ohhh!" Then they fell about giggling and laughing.

"No, Yolanda, she's not going to be one of my stable of girls, as you put it," Susanna replied sarcastically.

"Too right, I'm far too bossy for that," Mistress Chevalier agreed.

"Of course, Mistress Chevalier will have to live under my rules, and in my house, tardiness is not permitted," Susanna said.

"She was late yesterday, it took ages before we could get started," Mistress Yolanda pointed out.

"Yes, it did, and that is part of why I've decreed that Jade should get a good spanking before she comes to live here."

"Good idea," Baroness Carruthers said.

"About time, I'd say," Dame Cartwright agreed.

"Yes, it's long overdue!" Madam Cauldwell chimed in.

"No! Please, Mistress Susanna, I beg of you. Don't promise me a better place to live and work, and then require me to submit to this!" Mistress Chevalier protested.

"You beg? Is that how you beg for my forgiveness, Jade? Shouldn't you be on your knees if you're begging me?"

"Yes, get on your knees!" Mistress Yolanda agreed boisterously.

Jade muttered under her breath, but she dropped to one knee, "Oh great Mistress Susanna, please, forgive me for my tardiness."

"What do you think, ladies? Is that a sufficient apology?"

Some said no, but most recommended a punishment.

Susanna shook her head sadly. "It seems the ladies have spoken, Jade. If you want to join us here, you're going to get a spanking today. Now. In front of everyone."

"Please, no, don't."

"Stand here and bend over!" Susanna snapped. Mistress Chevalier stood up, looking defiant but stood where she was told and bent over, putting her hands on her knees.

"On the bare!" someone called out when they saw Jade's trousered bottom, and others added their agreement. "Yes, on the bare!"

"Yes, I think that's best, don't you, Jade?" Mistress Susanna replied.

"No, it's not. Strip her naked. A slut shouldn't keep her dignity when she's being punished, should she ladies?" the Baroness urged gleefully. The assembled ladies were easily swayed. They were baying for Mistress Chevalier to be punished properly, to see her humiliated as they would with a recalcitrant sub.

"Well, Jade? Are you going to take your own clothes off, or shall I have you stripped? I think I'll have enough volunteers."

"You wouldn't dare!" Jade said.

Susanna shook her head. "Enough. Ladies, strip her if you will."

With glee, several of the dommes got up on the stage and manhandled Jade. Two held her arms tight, while a third unbuttoned her blouse and jodhpurs. Then they pulled her trousers down around her ankles, and the shit off her back. Her underwear followed, and though she struggled, she didn't use her safeword or protest.

Soon, the tardy domme was left entirely nude.

"What shall it be, the pillory or a bench?" Susanna asked, counting the votes. "The bench it is then. Strap her down."

Susanna didn't bother with any preamble, once Jade was in position, she stepped forward and began to spank her with great big smacks that made her plump bottom jiggle and echoed around the room. Jade cursed like a sailor, as each blow connected with her big wobbly bottom, which was soon turning shades of bright pink.

"Ow. You bitch, Susanna!" Mistress Chevalier cursed, struggling against her bonds.

Susanna laughed. "Bitch, am I, Jade? I think that's earned you another two dozen, don't you?"

"Do your worst, I can take it!" Jade growled defiantly.

Susanna resumed spanking, laughing when Jade howled loudly each time her hand connected with her cheeks. "Jade is such a noisy slut! I think we need to keep her quiet," Susanna mused as her palm rhythmically pounded against the older woman's backside. "Vicky, kneel in front of her and shut her filthy mouth with your kisses, there's a good girl," Susanna ordered.

The muscular sub seemed happy with her orders and immediately complied, cupping Jade's head in her big hand and slipping her tongue into her domme's mouth. Jade still yelped and moaned as she was spanked, but Vicky muffled her quite effectively.

"Amber, kneel down behind her," Susanna said. When Amber had positioned herself, she asked, "Is she wet, Amber? Tell us all, if Jade is the slut she seems to be? Can you see signs that she's enjoying her punishment?"

Amber licked her lips, "Mistress Chevalier is really wet. She looks very aroused, Mistress."

"Let's see how my new Stable Mistress handles being punished while she orgasms, shall we?" Susanna suggested. "Amber, put your tongue to use."

Amber gratefully complied, burying her tongue immediately in Mistress Chevalier's wet folds, seeking out her clit as Susanna's hand descended again and again just above her head.

The tone and timbre of Mistress Chevalier's protests changed noticeably once Amber applied her lips and tongue to her task.

It was a source of considerable pride to Amber that she was able to make the experienced lesbian come so hard and so quickly, while she was being spanked. She masturbated to the memory quite frequently over the following months, even while being spanked herself.

When Susanna had finished, she pulled Amber up and kissed her, hungrily licking away the evidence of the multiple orgasms her sub had given Mistress Chevalier. "Good girl," she whispered in Amber's ear. As always, a thrill of pleasure coursed through Amber's body at the words. The approval of her mistress was a tangible reward to her now.

Susanna pushed Amber's shoulder down firmly, returning her to her knees, where she knew she belonged. She beckoned Sugar to her side, kissed her deeply, then whispered something in her ear, sending the maid scurrying from the room on an errand. Then she turned to the crowd to address them.

"To celebrate this happy occasion, when Mistress Chevalier agreed to enter my service so that we all might benefit from her skills as an artisan, and that I can improve my estate, I extend an offer for this gathering to continue until tomorrow evening. Who would like to stay?"

Amber was happy to see that everyone present was keen to stay another day, that meant a lot more chances to play with the guests.

Sugar returned in a hurry and handed Mistress Susanna the big purple strapon that Mistress Chevalier had used on Amber the previous afternoon. Sugar and Amber were instructed to help fit it to their domme, and when she was ready, Susanna got behind Mistress Chevalier and plunged the strapon deep into her.

"Vicky, come and watch your Mistress get fucked," Susanna ordered, summoning the ponygirl to her side to sit, entranced by the sight of the thick silicone cock filling her Mistress's wet pussy. "Thank you, Mistress Susanna," Vicky said gratefully.

"Would you like having your pussy licked, Vicky?" Susanna asked.

Amber was happy to oblige when Vicky said yes, and Susanna indicated that the task was her. She wriggled between Vicky's legs on her back, and the bodybuilding woman mounted her face with a satisfied sigh. Amber tongued her happily as the woman rode her face and watched her Mistress get fucked.

"What next? Sugar, apply your tongue to Amber's pussy. Candy, I want your tongue between my cheeks as I fuck Jade. If anyone wants to play with Sugar while she pleasures Amber, please feel free," Susanna said.

"I'd like to fuck Sugar," Baroness Carruthers said, as her sub, Charlotte, began to undress her so she could get into her strapon harness and join the party on the stage.

"Excellent! Please, ladies, this is a party. Enjoy yourselves!" Susanna said. After a second, clothes started to come off, submissives were bound to furniture, the sound of bottoms being punished and tongues being used for the purpose of pussy worship filled the room.

Amber found herself passed around like a box of luxury chocolates. Each dominant who received her unwrapped a different treat, before passing her on. Before a break for lunch was called, Amber had been taken in all holes, sometimes two at once. Her buttocks were as shockingly crimson as Mistress Chevalier's and her nipples were sensitive from the amount of licking and nibbling she'd enjoyed.

After lunch, Amber found herself lying back on one of the corner sofas. Mistress Susanna and Mistress Chevalier were on either side of her, fondling her breasts and plunging their fingers into her pussy together, as they chatted. Her thighs rested on Vicky's strong shoulders as she knelt on the floor. The ponygirl was using her tongue to pleasure Amber when their Mistress's fingers were elsewhere.

The powerful combination of sensations had Amber in an almost insensible state, as she reached climaxes one after another.

Mistress Chevalier lifted her head from another bout of nipple sucking and nibbling and grinned at Susanna. "My bum still hurts, you know."

"And don't you forget it, Mistress Chevalier," Susanna replied.

"I shall dream of returning the favour one day," Mistress Chevalier said.

"Keep dreaming."

"Do you think you'll try Amber out as a pony? I think she'd be wonderful, though I doubt she'd beat my Vicky," Mistress Chevalier asked.

Amber lifted her head from the cushions and protested, "Hey! I could beat, Vicky!"

"Don't interrupt, Amber," Mistress Susanna admonished her, roughly twisting her nipple and laughing as Amber yelped at the rough treatment before her head lolled back again as Vicky's tongue plunged back between her lips.

"I think it's certainly worth trying her out when the new stables are ready. Would you be interested in helping put Amber through some trials?" Susanna asked.

"I'd beat, Vicky," Amber mumbled. Then her head snapped up, and she screamed. "She bit me! Vicky bit me," she complained.

Vicky lifted her head and grinned wickedly, "Amber would never beat me, not in oil wrestling, and not in a pony race. She's too soft. Delicious, but soft."

"I am not. I bet I could take more strokes of the cane than you," Amber claimed.

"You can't even control your orgasms," Vicky said.

"I can control them," Amber boasted.

"Prove her wrong then, Vicky," Mistress Chevalier ordered, and her sub stopped talking and got back to worshipping Amber's pussy.

"How about we hold some pony trials then. Would you join us, Mistress Chevalier?" Susanna said.

"Vicky and I are in."

"Amber, would you like to try out as a pony?" Susann asked.

Amber's head collapsed back to the cushions again, as Vicky's tongue quickly proved her point. Amber was riding the wave of her second orgasm before she could muster the self-control to respond to her Mistress, who was patiently waiting.

"Yes, Mistress."

AUTHOR'S NOTE

Thank you for reading Shared by Her Lesbian Boss, Book Five of the Submissive Lesbian Personal Assistant series.

If you enjoyed the book and can spare the time to leave a review on Amazon or Goodreads, I would greatly appreciate it.

Positive and constructive feedback and comments, even a simple star rating, are a great way to let me know that you want to read more about these characters.

This series is about Amber, and the other women in service to Susanna Hamilton, a wealthy lesbian with a hedonistic lifestyle.

Miss Hamilton has a taste for games of domination and submission, and employs Amber to be her new Personal Assistant.

Amber has never gone beyond an active fantasy life, and actually played with another woman. Susanna offers the twin temptations of a much needed job and pleasures Amber has never tasted.

News and Updates

I'll be making some changes to my writing schedule for 2020. In 2019, I took on too many projects at once and it wasn't productive.

This year, I'm trying to stick to one or two at a time, and I aim to complete projects in order, one after the other. I have a spreadsheet, word counts, writing speed and costs worked out and everything!

If I can clear some of my backlog, I'll feel much happier and I hope, be able to increase my overall writing speed. That means more books for you to enjoy.

I've put some further detail below for anyone who cares to read it, chime in on Twitter about what you'd like me to be doing, or just find out what to expect.

Thanks, K.F. Jones

Amber and Susanna

Firstly, you may notice that this book is a little longer than previous entries in the series. The first book was 13.5k, the fourth jumped to 17.7k and this one is a whopping 27.4K!

That wasn't intentional, I just had too many ideas for the party itself and the sub-plot. There are also a far greater number of characters in this book. I'll do my best to keep book six, Driven by Her Lesbian Boss a bit shorter.

Driven will go into Amber's experiences trying pony play, with Mistress Chevalier and Mistress Susanna.

It will conclude the first story arc for Amber and Susanna and I hope to have it out in March (no promises, but positive encouragement will help with that).

Once that story arc is complete, I will release an omnibus edition of all six books for £9.99/$9.99 in Kindle ebook. I'll keep the paperback price as low as I can. Bought separately in ebook format, all six books would cost £17.94/$17.94.

I hope that is a reasonable discount to offer for those who do prefer to buy.

If price is an issue, the most cost effective way to read my books is to subscribe to Kindle Unlimited. That's how I read so much, I could simply never afford to read everything I do, if it I had to buy each book, rather than borrow it.

Once the omnibus is out, and my other projects have been finished or progressed sufficiently, I'd be thrilled to write a second arc in the main series of Amber and Susanna, if there's demand for it.

I really enjoy writing about Amber and Susanna, and I have plenty of ideas as to what they will get up to as their relationship develops.

Do I hear the cry of tropical birds on an island retreat for kinky lesbians? Perhaps the sound of bells, which could either signal a wedding, or a thoroughly deviant surprise some of our dominants have for their subs?

Remember, let me know what you want, because I promise, I will pay close attention to requests.

Amber's Culinary Adventures

I also have plans to write a series of short stories, Amber's Culinary Adventures. Don't worry, they're not actually about cooking. Here's some title ideas - see if they whet your appetite:

- A Dash of Pepper
- A Sprinkling of Sugar
- A Taste of Pudding
- A Filling of Ginger

The Culinary Adventures would be single scene, erotic shorts about an encounter Amber has with one or more of her friends.

The plan would be to release them as individual works, at the lowest price point Amazon allows, £0.99/$0.99. They would also be available in Kindle Unlimited.

When I have enough, I would then release an omnibus which will be the most cost effective way to read the stories if you don't subscribe to Kindle Unlimited.

If you prefer not to buy erotica short stories (this series is made up of novelettes and novellas for anyone who is curious) that's perfectly understandable.

At that price point, they're kind of loss leaders for me anyway due to the way Amazon's royalty structure works (that's not a complaint just something we consider when pricing).

What I expect is for readers to prefer to buy the omnibus edition of short stories instead, but I'll publish them individually too, rather than wait based on that assumption.

Here's a summary:

- A series of erotic stories about Amber
- Short, one or two scenes, 5K words
- $0.99/£0.99 individually
- Omnibus to follow
- Seven outlined so far!

One advantage these shorts would have, is that I can fit them in as palate cleansers (for me) between other writing projects.

Hellcats Academy - Izzy & Kaos

After that, I will release an omnibus edition and move on to other projects. I have two goals, finish several series I've started, and write a solid hit.

Carlotta Black and I are working (slowly I'm afraid) to revamp Enchant, our paranormal reverse harem romance about Izzy and Kaos. It's far too steamy for the average RH reader, but doesn't hit their interests correctly either!

We'll be rewriting book one completely. You'll meet the antagonists in the new first book, and they'll play a more prominent role.

Izzy is our main hero and needs to be the centre of attention, from the reader, not just her growing harem of sexy men.

Kaos and her harem will be taking a back seat, rather than playing an equal part in the main series. Kaos will remain in the main series as both a reluctant opponent in the contest, and a valuable ally against the antagonists.

Because I can't help myself, I'll be making sure to detail the life of Kaos as she recruits, trains, dominates, torments, and otherwise plays with her own harem. We'll release those works as a separate but consecutive erotica series for those of you who want the extra steamy bits and to know more about Kaos.

I do expect that this will take some months sadly, and we won't change anything until we can release books one and two, most likely.

Let Me Know What You Think

For those of you who have Kindle Unlimited, you can borrow all my books and, if you want to read them again at some point, you'll be able to borrow the omnibus editions so they don't use up lots of slots in your Kindle library.

Don't forget to let me know if you want me to prioritise writing more of the Lesbian Boss series, over say, finishing the Sexy Student Lessons series or adding another quartet to my Consort of the Werewolf King series.

I'm quite active on Twitter at the moment though it's not safe for work, so be warned.

It's a pretty good place to reach me as I write this (Feb 2020) if you want to support me, talk about the books, or let me know which of my series I should concentrate on.

Thanks for your support, and for buying the book or borrowing it through Kindle Unlimited.

Yours steamily,

K.F. Jones

ALSO BY K.F. JONES

The Consort of the Werewolf King is the first series by K.F. Jones and follows a young English biology student, who is bitten by a wild wolf.

His friends and colleagues insist that there are no wolves in the UK. William's hunt to prove he was not imagining things leads him to meet, Brian, a local landowner who may be more than he seems.

Consort of the Werewolf King

Bitten by the Alpha - Book 1

Claimed by the Alpha - Book 2

Trained by the Alpha - Book 3

Initiated by the Pack - Book 4

Other work by K.F. Jones

Dawn and the Galvanic Capacitor

Dawn and The Pilferer's Punishment

Dawn and the London Society

Dawn is a bounty hunter, bodyguard and private detective in a steampunk world full of adventure, excitement and lusty antics.

The Tribulations of Dawn will follow our heroine as she tries to reclaim a stolen item for her employer. The Professor is at the forefront of research into advanced steam technology, and his invention could change the world for good or ill.

Dawn has a wandering, and somewhat lascivious eye, to match her quick wit and mean right hook. Woe betide the thieves when she catches them.

But can she be well-behaved for long enough to safely return the gizmo to the Professor? Or will it slip through her fingers and send her off on the chase again?

Submissive Lesbian Personal Assistant

This is a new series about Amber, a young woman who is seduced by her new employer, a dominant and wealthy lesbian.

Punished by Her Lesbian Boss

Seduced by Her Lesbian Boss

Trained by Her Lesbian Boss

Raced by Her Lesbian Boss

ABOUT THE AUTHOR

K.F. Jones is writing in two main worlds. The first is about a young man who finds love in the arms of an older werewolf with a kinky streak. The Consort of the Werewolf King features some very naughty werewolves, that no amount of discipline will tame.

The second is all about strong, confident young women capable of taking on any challenge, in a sexy steampunk world. You'll meet Dawn first, and follow her as she tries to make up for a mistake made while she indulged her passions.

Later you'll meet Mercy, who should be studying at the Academy and concentrating on her exams. If she could just avoid regular disciplinary sessions in the Deputy Head's office, or find a way to keep the demanding Headmistress satiated, perhaps she could finally unravel the conspiracy she's discovered!

If you'd like to find out when new books are released, join the mailing list at the website. **http://kfjones.net/**

twitter.com/kfjonesauthor
facebook.com/KFJonesbooks
pinterest.com/kfjonesauthor
goodreads.com/kfjones
amazon.com/author/kfjonesbooks